Cra

Published by Loch Awe Press
P.O. Box 5481
Wayland, MA 01778

ISBN 9781940839073

Edited by Meghan Conrad
Cover Art by Caitlin Fry

Crashing the Net

Samantha Wayland

Also by Samantha Wayland

Destiny Calls
With Grace
Hat Trick Book One: Fair Play
Hat Trick Book Two: Two Man Advantage
Hat Trick Book Three: End Game

Dedication

For Serena Bell, master plotter and the queen of cognitive dissonance.

Acknowledgements

Any other editor would have taken this author out behind the barn and shot me for what I did in the course of writing, rewriting, and editing this book. Meghan Conrad has earned not only my deepest gratitude, but possibly sainthood for this one.

To all the other friends, beta readers, and innocent bystanders harmed in the making of this book, I offer my thanks and apologies. Particularly Stephanie Kay, for keeping me on deadline. Serena Bell, Dalton Diaz, and Victoria Morgan, for reading one version or another of this story more than once. And my family, for putting up with late nights and a whole lot of take-out for dinner.

Author's Note

This book takes place three years before the Hat Trick Series.

Chapter One

Mike Erdo had lived the first twenty-two years of his life without learning the taste or texture of sexual lubricant.

Until a moment ago, that had actually been a *regret*.

Standing in the door of the Moncton Ice Cats' locker room, his mouth full of absolutely revolting goop, he searched for a place to spit out the world's biggest artificial loogie before his gag reflex got the better of him.

Too late.

He shuddered and hocked it onto the floor.

At least, he hoped he hit the floor and not his own shoe. Or worse, someone else's shoe. He couldn't see a fucking thing through the gallons of lube still streaming down his face and over his shoulders. It dripped steadily from the fingertips of his right hand, so he used his comparatively clean left to gingerly wipe what he could away from his eyes.

God, it was *disgusting*.

His new teammates were doubled over with hysterical laughter. Several collapsed onto the benches and one guy even hit the floor. Mike, virtually shellacked in clear, viscous, faintly medicinal-scented fluid, worked hard to laugh right along with them.

Another huge glob of lube dripped from his nose to land on the floor with a splat of finality.

Maybe tomorrow would be less of a suckfest. It couldn't be worse than today. Or yesterday. Yesterday actually made today look pretty fucking fantastic.

A big hand landed on his shoulder, sending up a spray in all directions. Mike refused to wince, even as his vision blurred from the rush of pain.

"Welcome to the Ice Cats!"

"Thanks," he said brightly, acutely aware that all eyes were on him. He searched for something to say. To do. He'd wanted to make a good first impression, but he had no idea how the fuck was he supposed to roll with this.

His gaze fell to the enormous empty jugs a few feet away and the first *incredibly dorky* thought that popped into his mind actually flew out of his mouth. "I had no idea lube came in such large containers."

His teammates doubled up again. Someone fell headfirst into their locker.

Mike's cheeks burned, no doubt turning a god-awful shade of red. The guy still gripping his shoulder was laughing so hard, Mike practically vibrated from it. He turned to look at the man and his mouth fell open before he could think better of it, accidentally letting in more lube.

Holy shit, he's fucking hot.

The beautiful man grinned. Full lips, Deep dimples. Bright green eyes dancing.

"I am Alexei," the man announced, his Russian accent unmistakable even in those three little words.

I should have known.

Alexei's wide shoulders and chest, coupled with the insanely powerful thighs his worn jeans struggled to contain, should have been Mike's first clue he was looking at a goalie. And in the case of the Ice Cats, the metric ton of lube soaking into his clothes should probably have been a good hint, too. Alexei Belov was *infamous* for his pranks. Wild tales of locker rooms having to be repainted, decontaminated, and possibly even fumigated, were rampant in the league.

Mike tore his eyes away from the Alexei's pink lips and shit-eating grin and studied the puddle spreading around his feet. Maybe today wasn't so bad, after all. He still had all his teeth and he wasn't on fire. That was something, right?

He risked another glance at the god standing next to him and smiled weakly. "I'm Mike."

"We know," Alexei said with a chuckle. Then he cocked back his arm.

Mike knew what was coming and steeled himself, but it was a wasted effort. Nothing could sufficiently prepare him for Alexei's punch to his arm.

He staggered back.

Goddamn, that hurts.

Alexei stepped aside for the next player, and so began the ritual that Mike had been expecting and dreading all day. He'd done this to countless new teammates in the course of his life, but now he wondered why the fuck were hockey players all such assholes. One after another, the Wild Cats introduced themselves, then slapped his back, punched his arm, or, in a few cases, gave his ass a firm swat. Mike stood solid, discreetly taking deep breaths and ignoring the black spots dancing before his eyes.

He could get through this. He *would* get through this. He'd done this when he'd arrived at his last team, and the one before, and this was no different. He wouldn't have thought anything of it if they'd done this yesterday. Or a week from now. The men around him had no way of knowing how fucked up Mike was *today*, of all days.

An eternity later, they completed their special, violent, and unwittingly excruciating greeting. Mike took satisfaction that most of the guys left complaining that they had to go wash lube off their hands before they could go out for the night.

Serves them right.

Only Alexei and Garrick LeBlanc—who'd actually introduced himself, in case Mike had been living under a rock for the last ten years—stayed behind with him in the locker room.

Garrick cocked his head. "You okay?"

Mike smiled like he hadn't a care in the world. "Yeah, sure."

Garrick's dubious look made Mike think he needed to work on his carefree smile. Since that wasn't working, he took the next best option. Retreat.

He waved his hand toward the back of the room. "Showers that way? 'Cuz I don't think you want me showing up at the bar like this."

"Yeah, even Smitty's wouldn't let you in," Garrick agreed with a smirk.

Alexei snorted. "Not sure this one is old enough to drink anyway."

Mike rolled his eyes, but didn't take the bait. He was used to annoying comments about his age, even if the Russian accent made this one sound more charming than usual.

He hefted his gear bag up off the floor and grimaced at the puddle on top, praying the clothes within weren't as ruined as the ones he was wearing. As it was, he was going to leave a slug-trail of lube across the locker room, but it was either that or leave one between here and the parking lot, then do untold damage to the already crappy upholstery in his piece-of-shit car.

He barely bit back his sigh and forced another bright smile. "I'll see you guys later."

Garrick studied him and said nothing, so Mike looked at Alexei.

Damn. Still hot.

Alexei nodded. "Yeah, see you later, kid."

"Only if you're wearing your glasses, old man." *So much for not taking the bait.*

Alexei's eyes lit with amusement. Fortunately, Garrick's bark of laughter pulled Mike's attention away before he could start drooling.

"He's got your number, Belov."

"We'll see about that," Alexei replied in a slow drawl as he looked Mike over.

Mike turned away, afraid his stupid baby face would give away his every thought. And his dick was *definitely* going to give a few things away if Alexei kept looking at him like that. Mike focused on unloading his gear into his stall, dragging what should have been a five minute chore out for as long as possible.

It felt like hours before Alexei and Garrick finally left and Mike could collapse onto the bench behind him.

It was supposed to be one of the best days of his life. A new team. Professional hockey. His first time truly on his own, finally able to support himself and help his family, all without a parent hovering over his shoulder.

And that was good. Really good.

Maybe tomorrow it would even feel that way.

"Alexei!"

Alexei turned to see Garrick jogging across the parking lot toward him. "What's up?"

"The new guy...Mike? He, uhh..." Garrick shrugged.

Alexei sighed, once again nipped by the guilt he'd been actively ignoring since he'd pulled this evening's prank.

"Do you think he's all right?" Garrick asked.

"I'm sure he's fine."

"Yeah? He just seemed kind of..."

Lost? Hurt? Really fucking pretty?

"...overwhelmed."

Alexei's shoulders slumped. *Fuck.* He hadn't been imagining it. "Okay, I'll go back in. Check on him."

Garrick's eyes widened. "You sure?"

Alexei tried not to take Garrick's surprise personally.

13

Normally this was exactly the sort of thing Alexei would let Garrick handle. But there'd been something about that kid. Those goddamn eyes. Even when he'd been grinning and joking with the rest of them, he'd still seemed...*sad.*

Alexei blew out a deep breath. Occasionally, his pranks did backfire. He'd been trying, in his own admittedly perverse way, to welcome the newest member of the team. Not make him miserable. "No, it's cool. I'll go check on him. Make sure he knows where Smitty's is."

"I'll see you there, then?"

"Yeah, see you in a few."

Alexei trudged back into the arena, surprised to find the locker room empty. He almost left to continue his search in the gym or the offices when he heard the water running in the pitch black shower room.

Shit, what if the poor kid hadn't been able to find the light switch?

It took a few seconds for Alexei's eyes to adjust to the low light cast through the door from the locker room, but eventually he found the tall, rangy defenseman standing under a torrent of water on the far side of the showers. He had his hands planted on the tile wall, his head hanging down so the spray beat down on his neck and between his wide shoulders.

It was a damn nice view, but something wasn't right. Tremors racked Mike's body, his unsteady breaths audible even over the rushing water.

Alexei almost dove back into the locker room, desperate to call Garrick and beg him to come back. This so wasn't his fucking thing.

Don't be such a coward, Belov.

In a burst of stupid courage, he charged into the shower room, crossing the tile to the point where the toes of his boots darkened from the water splashing back up off the floor. He still didn't have the faintest fucking idea what he was going to say or do, but then he saw what the shadows and steam had hidden.

The kid was covered in bruises.

"Did we do that to you?" he demanded, picturing how the team had pounded on him.

Mike jumped, almost losing his footing on the wet tiles. He slapped a hand on the wall to steady himself. "Jesus! You scared the shit out of me!"

Alexei looked away from red-rimmed eyes and instead tried very hard not to notice how tempting Mike's long frame and whipcord muscles were, in spite of the colorful array of reds and purples blanketing him.

"Did we do that?" he asked again, gesturing to a particularly vivid patch of blue on Mike's shoulder. Right where Alexei had punched him. But not *that* hard. "Do you bruise super fucking easily or something?"

"What? No. I play hockey, for Christ's sake."

"I've seen a lot of hockey players naked, and none of them looked like this!"

Mike blinked water from his eyes and looked at Alexei like he was crazy.

Okay, so that really hadn't come out the way Alexei had meant it to.

Mike spared Alexei having to explain by turning away and ducking his head back under the shower. "What are you doing here?" he asked.

"Looking for you." *Looking* at *you*. Alexei let his gaze follow the streams of water down the long, lean back. *Man,* that ass was spectacular.

So...*biteable.*

Then he saw a distinctly boot-shaped bruise on the back of the kid's thigh. "What happened to you?"

"It's nothing."

"It sure as hell is *something*."

"No. It's not." He turned, his hands planted on his hips, his scowl fierce. "Not to you."

Alexei's brain went completely blank when he noticed Mike's junk was waxed clean.

Alexei went back to glaring at Mike's *face.* "Did you deserve it?"

"What?"

He indicated the bruises running down his ribs. "Were you an asshole? Did you start it?"

"*No.*"

Alexei believed him, if only because he sounded so offended.

"Then why did they do it?" Because no way just one person did that much damage.

"If I had any idea who the fuck they were, maybe I'd ask them."

Alexei's mouth went dry and for a moment he forgot about the fact that Mike was still standing there, stark naked, without a lick of modesty. "You were attacked by strangers?"

"Yeah, of course. Seriously, who do you even hang out with? I got jumped, okay?"

"When?"

"Last night. Look. Forget I said anything."

"But—"

"No. I don't even know why I told you that much." He turned to shut off the water, muttering under his breath, "I should have just made some shit up."

Alexei didn't move, forcing Mike to look up when he couldn't get around Alexei.

"You can trust me," Alexei said, as surprised by his earnest declaration as Mike appeared to be. Probably way *more* surprised than Mike.

16

"Okay," Mike said slowly. "Thank you. I'll bear that in mind. But for now, at least, can we please drop it?"

Alexei barely knew the guy, and it wasn't any of his business, but he didn't *want* to let it go. It fucking rankled, but he gave in, for now. "Fine."

Mike's shoulders slumped. "Thank you."

Alexei took a few head-clearing steps away, grabbed the towel from its hook, and tossed it to Mike. "Come on. I'll drive you to Smitty's."

"That's not necessary," Mike said, his voice muffled as he scrubbed his hair dry.

Alexei tried not to look too much, but it was fucking hard. He didn't breathe normally again until Mike wrapped the towel around his waist. He'd spent his entire life in locker rooms and never had this problem before. He took several more head-clearing steps back toward the locker room, but Mike followed.

"I don't think I'm going to make it out tonight. I'm not much for company, anyway."

Funny, Alexei wasn't feeling particularly social anymore, either. "I'll drive you home, then."

"Thanks, but I have a car."

"Need directions?" he asked, as if everyone didn't rely on GPS these days. What the fuck was the matter with him?

"No, I'm good. I'm crashing at the Fairmont Motel around the corner for a few days while I look for a place to live."

Alexei shuddered. "You'll get crabs."

"Sorry, what?"

"You'll get crabs. From the sheets. You know, itchy things in your—"

"*Oookay!* Got it. Thanks for the warning."

"You can stay with me." Alexei honestly couldn't believe the words coming out of his mouth.

Mike looked as alarmed as Alexei felt. "No, thank you. I

appreciate—"

"Yes. I have a guest room. It will be fine." He sounded like he was trying to convince himself as much as Mike. Which he was. Jesus Christ. This wasn't his thing. Garrick was the one who acted like some goddamn goodwill ambassador to anyone new in town. Alexei was the one who dumped lube on their heads by way of a greeting. That was how it was supposed to work.

Mike shook his head. "Really, I don't want to impose. Thank you anyway, though."

Damn kid was stubborn. Why did that make Alexei want to smile?

"I insist. I can help you find an apartment tomorrow. I know a place. Clean. Decent rent." *Safe.*

"Thanks, really, but my budget is probably too small for anything you have in mind."

Alexei knew roughly how much Mike was making, but he didn't ask where the money was going. Not his business. "This building will work. Now, come on. I still want a beer, even if it's at my place."

Mike hesitated. "You sure?"

The only thing Alexei was sure of was that he'd lost his damn mind. Even as he was nodding and telling Mike he was more than welcome, Alexei was calculating how to get Mike's enticing ass back out of his apartment as quickly as possible.

Chapter Two

Mike sat in the cab of Alexei's gigantic pickup truck, trying to make sense of the deserted warehouse looming above of them. He thought Alexei had been taking them to Alexei's home, but he'd driven them here. Now, large steel doors slowly parted to reveal a huge, barren cavern, lit only by their headlights.

Alexei drove inside, parked and hit the remote to close the doors behind them. He plucked a foot-long Maglite from his glove box and jumped from his truck.

"Come on."

Mike grabbed his bag and chased the beam of Alexei's flashlight to the back corner of the building and an ancient industrial elevator that could easily have fit Mike's mid-sized Toyota inside.

"Where the hell are we going?"

Alexei laughed. "You'll see."

At least the lift had a light. That was about all it had going for it, though. It rattled and swayed alarmingly as it delivered them up to the fourth floor. Mike had to focus on not squeaking like a little girl with every jolt. Finally, they came to a stop and Alexei pried open the enormous doors.

Mike stared down a long hallway made of partially finished walls draped in plastic tarps, illuminated by bare bulbs hanging from the ceiling.

What the fuck is this place?

Every horror movie Mike had ever watched replayed in his head. It was surely a coincidence that the psycho killer in those Halloween movies wore a goalie mask, right?

He trailed Alexei down the hallway, painfully aware that he was the new guy in town who'd stupidly followed a man he didn't know right to his lair. And no one knew where he was. Or who he was with. Surely Alexei wouldn't carve him up into little pieces and leave the Ice Cats' defense down a man. Right?

They arrived at a wide, steel door.

The kind you could claw at for months and never get out.

"This is my house," Alexei announced. He threw the heavy door open and all Mike's worries over his pending demise disappeared.

Before him was a huge kitchen, gleaming with granite countertops and stainless steel appliances, including a stove that somehow suited the name emblazoned across the front—*Viking*. A wall of windows looked out across the city streets to the river and reflected the light of the funky fixtures above the kitchen table and counters—all suspended from the heavy steel girders holding up the twenty-foot ceiling above.

To the right was the living room, vaguely separated from the dining room by the enormous sectional couch and the sheer amount of space around the enormous table. Reading lamps, wood floors, and area rugs made what should have been a harsh, industrial space welcoming.

"Come on, I'll show you where to throw your stuff," Alexei said.

Mike snapped his mouth shut—how long had he been standing there with it hanging open?—and followed Alexei down a hallway. They walked past an office, a bathroom with a cool glass-block shower, a bedroom with a gigantic bed that Mike wasn't going to think about again—much—and on to a smaller bedroom.

"You can crash here."

Mike dropped his bag. "Thanks. This place is great."

"Thank you," Alexei said with a smile. "I just moved in."

Mike wanted to ask how Alexei had found such a bizarre and amazing home, but didn't want to seem rude or nosey. Mike was definitely going to have to apartment hunt on his own, though, because if this was what Alexei was used to, the place he had in mind for Mike would probably be way outside his budget.

Alexei walked back to the kitchen and went straight for the fridge. He needed a beer.

Grabbing two, he opened them both and plunked one down on the counter. "Here. Just don't tell the cops I'm corrupting a minor."

Mike stopped gaping at the stove and shot Alexei a dirty look. "I'm twenty-two."

Ten years younger than Alexei. "All right, kid. Then there's your beer. You had supper?"

"No, the nursery only gave me a bottle and some gruel before they sent me to the arena."

Alexei stuck his head back into the fridge and smirked. The kid had some grit.

"How about an omelette?"

"Uh…sure."

Alexei looked over his shoulder. "You could try to sound less surprised that I know how to cook."

"I just figured it must have been tough to learn when you were young. What with dinosaur eggs being so big and all."

Alexei laughed. Definitely some grit. He grabbed the ingredients he needed to make dinner and put it all on the island. He shoved the peppers, a knife and a cutting board at Mike. "Here, chop these. Then you can set the table."

"Okay, Dad."

Alexei barely suppressed a shudder. "*Don't* call me that." His eyes dipped to where Mike's T-shirt clung to his flat belly and tight abs. Alexei wasn't feeling in the least bit paternal.

"Sorry," Mike said, his laughter gone.

Shit, now he had that sad-eye thing going again. Alexei

fucking hated it. He yanked out the drawer full of his cast-iron pans and it squealed in protest.

Alexei got an idea. Wiping the smirk from his face, he turned to his houseguest. "Hey, can you come here a minute?"

Mike put down his knife and circled the counter. "Yeah?"

"This drawer is squeaking."

Mike hesitated at his side. "Okay. What can I do to help?"

Alexei grabbed the taller man in a headlock and dug his fingers behind Mike's ears.

"What the hell are you *doing*?" Mike protested, shoving at him before standing up all the way and almost lifting him off his feet.

Alexei held on for all he was worth. The kid was *strong*. "Hold still. I need some lube. I bet you've still got some back here somewhere."

Mike's laughter echoed off the high ceilings. "Yeah, and whose fault would that be, Belov?"

Alexei grinned. "Yours, newbie."

Mike woke up the next morning and couldn't remember where the hell he was. Not that this was anything new. He'd been traveling with one team or another for years, and waking up in bizarre hotel rooms was pretty standard.

But this didn't look like a hotel room. And he swore he smelled someone cooking French toast.

Then he remembered.

Alexei.

Mike flopped onto his back and scrubbed his hands through his hair, trying not to conjure up an image of his host, nor vividly recall the night they'd spent on his couch drinking beer, watching hockey, and just shooting the shit. At some point, Alexei had stretched his arm out along the tall cushions, just to get comfortable, and Mike had fought the urge to lean into the long curve of his body, acutely aware of how big the couch was and how he'd chosen to sit right next to Alexei.

He could only assume Alexei was being polite when, after getting them another round, he'd returned to the same spot instead of choosing a more appropriate seat on the other side of the sectional.

Mike huffed and sat up in bed, glaring balefully down at his stubbornly enthusiastic morning wood, willing it to subside.

It took a while and a focused and detailed mental review of the childbirth video he'd been forced to watch in eighth grade biology class.

Worked every time.

Jumping from the bed, he threw on his clothes and followed the amazing smells to the kitchen.

He found his host standing at the stove, his bare back to the door. Flannel pajama bottoms barely clung to his hips and the smooth swell of his ass. Mike stared hungrily at the twin dimples hovering on either side of Alexei's spine, forgetting to breathe until his lungs seized up and he made a small choking sound.

Alexei turned.

"Good morning," Mike gasped, hoping like hell his voice sounded just-woken-up scratchy and not like he'd swallowed his tongue. Because *damn*, the view from the front was even better.

"Good morning." The rough timbre of Alexei's voice rubbed over Mike's skin, making the hairs on the back of his neck prickle.

This was *so bad.* He needed to get a handle on himself.

Mike had known since the first blush of puberty that he was gay. When the guys had started talking about girls, he'd still been thinking about the guys. And from there it had only gotten more obvious.

To him, anyway. Everyone else just saw a hockey player.

Which, apparently, meant "straight guy."

It had taken a long time for him to really accept that he wanted something different than what was expected of him. And truth be told, what he wanted more than anything or anyone else he'd ever met, was standing right in front of him.

Which really only proved he was a fucking idiot. Anyone would think he'd learned his lesson after what had happened in Quebec City the night before last, but Alexei made him want to forget.

It was way more than that body, too—spectacular though it was. Or the vivid green eyes and curling brown hair, which was wild with bed-head and just fucking *begging* Mike to run his fingers through it.

It was that Alexei looked right at him. When Alexei talked, joked, just checked to see if Mike wanted some orange juice, he never failed to catch Mike's gaze. He didn't talk at Mike, he spoke *to* him. *Saw* him.

Last night they'd talked about shit that *wasn't* hockey, which was so unusual for Mike that he'd stumbled through the first half hour of the conversation. Thankfully, the game on TV had held Alexei's attention so that he couldn't see Mike's red cheeks and twitchy hands.

But then Alexei had asked him about home, pretending not to notice when Mike went on about his sister, Jayne, and how proud he was of her. They talked about his last team. How long ago Alexei had come over from Russia, completely alone, at age eighteen. Alexei had been surprised Mike's father had moved to Kingston with him, but hadn't gotten that look in his eye. The one that said Mike was a loser for living with his dad until he was twenty-two years old. Alexei hadn't even questioned it when Mike said it hadn't been his idea, nor his preference, but that his dad wasn't one of those psycho hockey-dads. Not really.

Alexei understood just how fucking great it was that Mike was on his own now. He had teased him for not being able to cook anything more complicated than a grilled cheese and his plan to live on protein shakes until he could learn. And nothing beat Alexei's glee when Mike had admitted he liked to play chess, even if in the same sentence he'd had to confess he sucked at it. His tongue had been tied in knots, his chest tight, as Alexei leaned into him to point out the marble chess set on its own little table across the room.

This morning over breakfast the subject *was* hockey, and that was proving to be almost as foreign an experience as last night had been. Mike, of course, had spent most of his life either playing or talking about the sport, but this was different. Alexei asked him questions and listened to his answers. Like he cared. Like he believed what Mike said without checking with a coach or glancing at Mike's father, always over Mike's shoulder. Until now. And fuck, why hadn't Mike figured out just how much he'd learned up until now? What he knew. Because after two hours of debating everything from the best way to tape a stick, to whether or not Sidney Crosby was hockey's version of the Second Coming, he realized it was a hell of a lot. And Alexei—he looked like he respected that. Like he might want to talk more about shit like this.

Mike had never felt less *invisible.*

Which was a bitch, since he had to keep hiding who he really was for all he was worth.

Somehow, Mike managed to get through breakfast without embarrassing himself, mostly thanks to the table concealing the unfortunate fit of his sweatpants whenever he looked too long at Alexei. Hell, he pitched a tent worthy of the LL Bean catalog when Alexei had leaned forward, his gaze narrowed as he tried to make his point. Mike had happily argued right back, confident that his message, his idea, would be heard.

He would have gladly sat here talking all day, priapism be damned. Which meant, of course, he probably should go.

Alexei seemed to have the same idea, though Mike didn't doubt it was for a different reason. Less than an hour after they'd cleaned up breakfast, Mike was signing the lease on a studio apartment a few blocks from Alexei's warehouse. The building was clean and safe, and the rent was insanely cheap. Mike suspected Alexei had convinced the building manager to give him a good deal, but he wasn't going to look a gift horse in the mouth and ask how.

New keys in hand, he and Alexei left to retrieve his car from the arena lot. He spent the first half of the drive telling himself not to read anything into the fact Alexei had opened the car door for him.

He couldn't pretend he didn't like it, though.

They pulled up beside his car in the parking lot and Alexei eyed the old Toyota, stuffed to the gills with boxes and dwarfed by Alexei's truck. Mike wondered when he'd started to think of big trucks as being sexy.

Alexei's voice cut into his wandering thoughts. "Where are you storing your furniture?"

"I don't have any yet. I'll have to go shopping over the next couple weeks."

"Where will you sleep?"

"I have a sleeping bag."

Mike had one hand on the door handle, about to thank Alexei and make his escape, when Alexei hit the gas and pulled back out onto the street.

"Where are we going?" Mike asked.

"Shopping."

Mike kept his eyes glued to the road as heat crawled up his neck and into his cheeks. He had no money. Like, *none*. His plan had been to buy a blow-up mattress at Target. That and the stuff in his car would get him through the first few months. "You don't have to do that. I'll take care of it later."

Alexei kept driving as if Mike hasn't spoken.

Mike discreetly pulled out his phone and tried to

determine how much room he had on his credit card.

Shit shit shit.

In his panic, it took Mike a while to notice they'd left the city.

His over-active imagination allowed his serial killer highlight reel to run through his mind again, even as he smirked at the absurdity of it. Alexei would never hurt him.

He was about to ask what stores were out this way when Alexei turned into a massive storage facility. Concrete bunkers lined with garage doors stretched as far as the eye could see.

"What are we doing here?"

Alexei parked in front of a large door and jumped from his truck. "Come on."

Mike followed, confused, and stood by while Alexei rolled open the storage unit door. Mike was still trying to sort out what the hell they were doing when Alexei gestured for him to help. With a few tugs, they pulled a full-size bed frame from the pile, soon followed by a mattress and box spring, a dresser, two lamps, a couch, and a decent area rug.

"What is all this stuff?" Mike asked, afraid the answer was obvious.

"Yours," Alexei replied gruffly.

"I can't."

Alexei pinned him with his sharp green gaze. "You will."

When Mike opened his mouth to protest, Alexei waved it off.

"Use this until you get your own stuff. I don't need it, as you can see."

"But—"

"Michael."

At Alexei's stern command, a wholly inappropriate curl of arousal unfurled in Mike's belly. He loved the way Alexei's accent added a lilt to his name, particularly since this was the first time Alexei had called him anything other than *kid*.

He opened his mouth, but his voice cut off when Alexei wrapped his big, warm hand around the back of his neck.

"Shut up."

"Okay."

Chapter Three

Mike spread his knees, stuck his ass in the air, and did his frog stretch. Just like he had done on the ice before every game since he could remember. Just like he would again in a week's time when he returned to Moncton. It didn't make any difference that they were in Quebec City. That he hadn't been here since he'd stopped on this way to Moncton, his plans for that night having gone terribly wrong.

Nor did it matter that it was the day before Christmas Eve and his father had come to watch the game, and then to drive Mike home afterwards for their short holiday break. A few days off should have been something to look forward to, but for Mike, it would be his own little hell.

He kicked out his right leg and gritted his teeth when his groin pulled, just a little. He needed to stop his brain and focus before he hurt himself. Or worse, fucked up this game.

He finished his stretches carefully, counting his breaths and calming his mind as he prepared to jump to his feet. Every game-night for the four months he'd been with the Ice Cats, there'd been one more step in his pre-game routine. It wasn't exactly what anyone would call standard practice. No one else on the team even knew about it, or if they did, they hadn't said a word. Probably didn't know what it meant. Hell, *Mike* didn't know what it meant. But it was the one thing—more than practice, conditioning, pep talks from the coach, or years of playing—that got him ready to bring his best to the game.

He cut his eyes to the goal and found Alexei patiently waiting. His lips twitched, then he winked.

Mike's heart lurched, just like always.

I'm a fool.

He and Alexei were friends. Close friends, but that was *all* they were. It was a lecture he gave himself on an almost daily basis anymore. When they watched a game together from their customary spots right next to each other on the couch. When they went out with the team and were smashed together in the corner booth of one bar or another. When Mike leaned his elbows on the table, laughing with his friends and teammates and trying not to feel the heat of Alexei's arm stretched across the back of his chair.

He didn't harbor any delusions that Alexei would ever be interested in him as anything other than a teammate, drinking buddy, and chess opponent. But Mike couldn't seem to stop his growing affection—layered on top of the instant attraction—for his friend.

So the wink mattered. Probably too much.

Definitely. Definitely too much.

He shook off his thoughts—ones he wouldn't usually allow to disrupt his focus before a game, though god knew they were a constant companion off the ice—and slid into the warm up drills. He focused on the feel of his skates beneath him as he circled the goal, making and catching passes, and joining the team as they put Alexei through his paces and limbered up their arms.

Christ, it was going to be a long drive back to Saguenay. His dad would have questions. Perfectly innocent ones that any father would ask. Was Mike seeing anyone? What was her name? Hours of torture in the car because his father wanted to catch a game and spend time with his son. Which was a good thing. Or it should be. Mike's dad was proud of him.

But that still didn't mean Mike could tell him the truth.

His last practice shot on the net went so wide, Alexei paused to look at him and let another two sail by.

Mike scolded himself to focus on the game. The ice. His team. He shouldn't be remembering what it had been like to be home for the whole month of July—a mistake he'd never make again. His mother's veiled hints about how much she looked forward to having grandchildren. His father constantly nudging him to go out and meet a "nice girl". Even Jayne, with her offers to hook him up with her friends.

It drove him crazy, and the harder he resisted, the harder they pushed. At least, his parents did. Jayne, at some point over the summer, had stopped asking. He'd wondered if she'd finally begun to clue in until he overheard her telling a friend she was convinced he was hiding a girl he didn't want the family to know about. Yet.

Well, she got it partly right. He was definitely hiding something. And the worst part was, he knew he should tell her the truth. Tell them all the truth. But he was a chicken. He didn't want to see the looks on his parents' faces when he broke their hearts. There would never be a big white wedding in their church. Or a daughter-in-law who would be thrilled to take his grandmother's china. Probably no grandkids for his father to play catch with or to take out on the ice.

So he kept silent. And they kept pressuring him, not knowing that every time they declared their interest in seeing him happy, they made him miserable.

He'd almost come out once, the need to shout the truth choking him in the final days he'd been home before joining the Ice Cats. Instead, he'd left for Moncton a day early and quietly checked into a hotel here in Quebec City for the night. Frustration and curiosity had finally pushed him to take a risk. To wander Rue Saint-Jean and the surrounding streets, just a couple miles from where he was tonight, until he found a quiet bar with a little rainbow flag tucked in the corner of the window.

And that sure as hell hadn't ended up the way he'd hoped.

Mike shuddered and stumbled into the bench, landing with a jarring thud. He nodded in response to Garrick's questioning look, trying to smile reassuringly. Based on the way Garrick's eyebrows rose beneath his helmet, Mike's fake smile still needed some work.

Even worse, it was two minutes until game time and Mike's focus had officially left the building.

Alexei stood ready in the net, watching his exhausted team battle into overtime, and knew that no matter what else was going on, his eyes should be absolutely glued to the puck.

He glanced at Mike again.

Something was wrong. Alexei didn't know what, but Mike wasn't right. Shoulders up, mouth grim, holding his stick way too tightly. It wasn't just the drag of overtime. Alexei had known something was up the moment they'd made eye contact during the warm up.

A fact he'd been obsessing over ever since.

In all his years playing the game, Alexei had never known a more reliable, steady player than Mike. The guy was a fucking rock. Except tonight.

Alexei itched to figure out what was going on. And no, it wasn't any of his business, but he was going to butt in anyway. The Ice Cats just needed to score. Hell, at this point, Alexei almost didn't care if the other guys scored. The game just needed to be *over*.

His eyes followed the puck, as they fucking well should, as it sailed across the ice. Mike caught it on his blade, set it, and with a mighty swing, shot a rocket from the point.

Goal!

Alexei exploded from the net as the team crashed into Mike, their gloved hands banging on his helmet as he grinned. Alexei slammed into the pile and Mike turned, opening a space and wrapping his arm around Alexei's waist. Pulling him in tight.

The now-familiar zing to Alexei's nuts hardly distracted him as their helmets clashed, Mike's eyes dancing as more players joined the pile-on. They could bury them under the entire team and all Alexei would feel was *Mike*.

It was a real fucking problem for Alexei these days. And as much as he hated it, he had a solution in mind. This holiday break, come hell, high water, or province-wide gay man shortage, Alexei was going to get laid.

For reasons he refused to dwell on, he couldn't bring himself to do it while Mike was around. But for the next few days, Mike would be gone and Alexei wouldn't hesitate.

Much.

With a final whap to Mike's perfect ass, Alexei sent him toward the locker room. Mike was all smiles, the haunted look lost to the glow of victory, until his eyes strayed up into the stands.

It was like watching a light go out.

Goddamn it, Alexei *would* figure out what the hell was going on.

Mike, though, didn't make it easy. He practically sprinted into the showers, barely rinsed off, and was dressed, hair still wet and standing up in all directions, before Alexei had even stepped *into* the damn showers.

Alexei u-turned and threw on his clothes without rinsing off. He stank, but he didn't give a fuck. Mike was gone before Alexei could pull on his damn shoes. He hadn't even said goodbye. And Alexei knew he wasn't going to be back at the hotel later, since he was headed home from here. Tonight.

Merry fucking Christmas to you, too, Mike.

Alexei stormed out of the locker room and turned toward the voices he heard from around the bend in the corridor.

"You won that one. You should celebrate."

"No, it's okay. I just want to get going. It'll be super late when we get home anyway. Where are you parked?" Mike asked.

Alexei stopped, still out of sight. He hadn't realized Mike's father was at the game, though in hindsight it was obvious that he would be. But why hadn't Mike mentioned it? Or introduced him to the guys, instead of tearing out of here like the place was on fire?

"Your mom will be happy to see you. And if we get going, I was going to ask if you already have plans for tomorrow night. I was talking to Bill down at the store and his daughter has been asking about you. You remember Sarah?"

Alexei thought he heard Mike sigh. "Of course I do, Dad. We went to school together."

"Great. Maybe you two could go out tomorrow. She's around and—"

"I don't think so, Dad."

"Why not, son? She's a nice girl."

"I'm sure she is. It's just I'm not—she's not—"

"*Oh*," Mike's dad drawled out, clearly having just come to some realization. "Are you seeing someone? I didn't even think to ask. I figured you would have told us."

Alexei crept forward, his stomach churning as he waited for Mike's answer. He was sure he would know if—

"*Dad*," Mike said patiently, though Alexei could hear he was annoyed. "I'm not seeing anyone. It's just..."

"There's someone special, isn't there?"

For a long time Mike didn't answer. Alexei held his breath.

"Yeah," said Mike on a long sigh. "I guess you could say that."

Mike didn't sound happy about it. In fact, he sounded incredibly sad.

Alexei felt kind of nauseous. For a lot of reasons.

Mike's father was either stupid or deaf, though, because he said, "Really?" with undisguised happiness.

"Yes. No." Another sigh. "Look, I don't want to talk about it, okay?"

"Sure, son. Let's go home."

"Great."

And with that one word, Alexei knew without a doubt that was the last thing Mike wanted to do.

"*Mike!*"

Alexei's way-too-loud shout bounced off the walls as he ran down the corridor toward Mike and his father. He racked his brain for an excuse for his abrupt interruption as he bounded around the corner and skidded to a halt at Mike's side.

His first thought was that he would have recognized Mike's father immediately. He was an older, slightly grayer, version of Mike.

Mike, on the other hand, didn't look like himself at all. His face was pale except for two bright red spots on his cheeks, and Alexei couldn't tell if he was terrified or relieved to see him. Maybe both.

Mike's father looked at his son with a confused smile.

"Uh, Dad. This is Alexei Belov, our goalie. Alexei, this is my father, John Erdo."

Alexei thrust out his hand. "Sir. It is pleasure to meet you," he said in his thickest Russian accent.

Mr. Erdo shook his hand with a nod, his narrow gaze shifting back and forth between Mike and Alexei.

"Mike, I need speak with you," Alexei blurted out. "Very important."

If he hadn't been so rattled, he might have laughed at the utterly bemused expression on Mike's face. Alexei hated pulling his *Russkiy* routine without warning Mike, but hoped he'd play along. People were generally intimidated by the prospect of conversing with someone who was difficult to understand. The last thing he wanted was for Mike's dad to strike up a conversation.

He hooked his hand around Mike's elbow and tugged. "Come, we go."

"Uh, okay. I'll be right back, Dad, then we can get going."

Mike's father nodded curtly, obviously still confused. And who could blame him? Alexei had no idea what the fuck he was doing either.

Mike tried, and failed, to yank his arm free. His cheeks burned with humiliation as he was unceremoniously marched into an empty office. There was no way Alexei hadn't heard Mike's incredibly stupid admission that there was someone special.

God, his heart had nearly stopped when Alexei's voice had rung out while Mike was still wondering what the fuck he'd been thinking to say something like that to his father.

The moment his arm was released, Mike stepped back. "What's with the crazy accent, Boris?"

"What's wrong?"

"Nothing is wrong. Except you sounding like the bad guy in a Bullwinkle episode."

"Why are you rushing out of here?"

"Apparently so my father can fix me up with every single woman in Saguenay," Mike blurted out before clamping his mouth shut.

"Why?"

"He and mom are tired of waiting for grandchildren." Mike saw how Alexei's eyes widened and almost cracked a smile. "I'm joking. Mostly." *Not really.*

"Why the hurry, Mike?"

"I don't know. I'm eager for some father-son bonding time?" And why the fuck did Alexei care anyway?

Alexei studied his face. "You don't want to go, do you?"

"I love my family," Mike said, and Alexei immediately nodded. For some damn reason it make Mike feel better that Alexei knew that. Believed it. So really, there was little point in lying about the rest. "But no. I don't really want to go home."

"Then come back to Moncton with us."

Ignoring the fact that Mike had already told the team he wouldn't need a hotel tonight, nor the flight home tomorrow, there were still tons of reasons it wasn't possible. Mike ruthlessly crushed the hope that had sprung to life just by Alexei mentioning it. "I can't. My dad is here already and my mom would be upset. I'm pretty much stuck unless I've got a game or another job."

Or get a pair and tell my family the truth. Then, he'd bet, he could spend his holidays however he chose, rather than sitting next to his mom at midnight mass.

Mike shivered remembering those weeks at home last summer. His only respite had been volunteering on the construction crew for the new rectory at his mom's church. Well, if it could be considered a respite to spend all day with people who thought homosexuality was an affront to god, and a foreman who blamed "those fucking faggots" for everything from the price of sheetrock to global warming.

Mike was so lost in the memory, he failed to notice Alexei's curious look.

"Why would you need another job? You have a good one with the Ice Cats."

Crap. The last thing Mike wanted to get into was his family's financial issues and his role in creating them. It must have been pretty fucking obvious by whatever expression was on his face, too. Alexei held up a hand before Mike could try to explain.

"Never mind. We'll talk about that later. Now, we find you work," Alexei said with a shrug.

As if it were that easy. "I don't have a job and no one is going to hire me for a week." Particularly since the only thing he knew how to do was play hockey.

"I will."

"What are you talking about? You going to pay me to clean your house or something?"

Alexei snorted. "I've seen your housekeeping. No, thank you. But you can help me build out the apartment next to mine this week."

"But, I don't know how to—"

"I'll teach you."

Alexei appeared to be completely serious.

Mike didn't get it. "Dude, is your landlord giving you cheap rent in exchange for slave labor or something?"

Alexei smiled. "Dude, I *am* the landlord."

Mike stared at Alexei, clearly shocked. He couldn't honestly believe he'd told Mike the truth either. Why was it with Mike, he always felt like he was flying by the seat of his pants?

"You own that building?" Mike asked with a level of amazement that wasn't entirely flattering to Alexei *or* the building.

"Yes. And three others." *Might as well lay out all my secrets.*

"Three others?" Mike paused, his eyes narrowing. "Do I happen to live in one?"

Alexei grimaced. "Ummm...yes?"

He'd expected Mike to be angry or annoyed. Surprised. The hurt in Mike's eyes, his voice, unearthed things in Alexei that were best left buried. "Why didn't you tell me?"

"I don't like to tell people my business," Alexei snapped, wincing when Mike jerked back. "Until now, okay? Now you're the only one who knows, besides my property managers and the bank."

Mike blinked. Then smiled crookedly.

It was stupid how happy this made Alexei.

"Why?" Mike asked.

"Why do I own buildings?" Alexei shrugged. "You know my father is a slumlord in Moscow. Maybe it's in my blood."

Mike wrapped a hand around his neck and jerked him close, startling Alexei. "Don't say that. You're a good person."

More happy and stupid burst to life in Alexei. He needed to get a handle on the shit Mike churned up in him.

But boy, did it please Alexei to see how Mike had come into his own. The kid he'd first met would never have gotten in his face. He liked this man even better.

Which was one of the many reason why self-preservation dictated that Alexei should keep Mike at arm's length. But that didn't come close to overriding his need to help Mike stay in Moncton for the holidays—and a few hundred miles away from his father and the women of Saguenay—if that was what he wanted.

Mike released Alexei's neck. "Let's try that again. *Why* do you own all these buildings?" he asked patiently.

"I don't want to go back to Moscow. I want to stay in Canada. In Moncton. I got my citizenship a couple years ago, and it helped to show I had a productive reason to be here once hockey is over."

Mike looked like he had a thousand questions, and Alexei realized with a shock that he was willing to answer them.

"Okay," Mike said at last.

"Okay?"

"Yeah, okay." Then he added, "Thank you for telling me."

"You're welcome." Sort of. Because while Alexei didn't regret it, he also wondered if he was making a huge mistake by letting Mike in. He plowed forward anyway. "So, will you come back and spend the holidays in Moncton with me?"

Alexei hadn't meant for it to sound quite so intimate, but it was worth it when the haunted look finally left Mike's eyes. "Yeah, I'll take the job. I just need to smooth things over with my dad."

"I'll come with you."

"No, you better take Boris back to the locker room before someone busts you for that bullshit. I'll come find you in a few minutes."

Alexei laughed, agreeing, and told Mike what he'd pay him for the week. Mike's eyes widened, but his shoulders also came down from around his ears, confirming Alexei's suspicion that the money would ease the way with his dad. Alexei swore to himself he'd find out why eventually.

When Mike went back down the hallway toward his father, Alexei pretended to go the locker room, waiting in the doorway until Mike wouldn't see Alexei following him.

"No way," Mike's father said.

"It's a good job, Dad. I'll send you a third, like always. It will help with Jayne's tuition. It's enough to pay for her books and then some."

Mike's father hemmed and hawed, until Mike told him a sum that was a hell of a lot closer to *two thirds* of what Alexei had offered.

Mike's father agreed.

Alexei slipped back into the locker room with a confusing mixture of anticipation and dread churning in his gut.

Chapter Four

Of course, deciding to blow off his family and go back to Moncton meant a host of logistics issues to deal with. Fortunately, Mike was able to get a ticket on his team's flight the next day, and they were only going to make him pay the difference in the airfare. Unfortunately, there were no rooms left at the team's hotel.

Standing in the lobby, Mike looked out onto Rue Saint-Jean and shivered. He really, really didn't want to go back out there. And not just because it was really freaking cold.

"You okay?"

Mike turned to Alexei. "Sure, just dreading the prospect of trolling for a place to sleep tonight." Which was the truth. Mostly.

"You can crash in my room."

Mike didn't hesitate. "Okay."

He hoped his relief wasn't obvious. Alexei was studying his face again, so he turned and staggered toward the elevators under the weight of his bags, all of which he'd already lugged to the arena and back.

Alexei took his large equipment back from his shoulder and left him with only his suitcase. Normally, Mike would object to that, but his brain felt scattered in a million directions, so he let it go. He remained silent for the elevator ride, ignoring Alexei's scrutiny. As they walked down the hallway toward Alexei's room, Mike could remember every decision he'd made that night, but he still couldn't quite figure out how he'd ended up here.

Alexei fished his keycard from his pants pocket and Mike definitely didn't watch how the fabric strained across his belly and thighs.

When the lock flashed, he pushed his way into the room and dropped his bag before coming to a halt and staring at the one king-sized bed.

"Oh," he said, brilliantly articulate as always.

"Is that a problem?" Alexei asked from behind him.

Why would it be? Mike thought somewhat hysterically. Guys crashed together all the time and the bed was practically big enough to fit a third person anyway.

"No problem. I just feel bad that I'm taking up half your bed."

Alexei chuckled. "I promise not to molest you while you're sleeping."

Mike laughed, maybe a little too loudly, and bent to open his suitcase. Thank fucking Christ he'd packed pajamas for home.

"You want to go out with the guys?" asked Alexei.

Mike froze. *Shit.* He really didn't want to see any more of Quebec City than the inside of this hotel room and whatever was out the bus's windows on the way to the airport, but he couldn't tell Alexei that.

"No, I'm good. Tired. I think I'll just stay in tonight." He looked over his shoulder at Alexei. "If that's okay with you, I mean? I know it's your room, so if you don't want me here while you're out—"

Alexei put his hand over Mike's mouth. "What is the matter with you?"

"What? Nothing," Mike said when he could speak again.

"You're being weird."

"I'm not. I just. I don't want to go out, okay?"

Alexei had spent so much of the past couple hours studying Mike's face, Mike was starting to feel like a specimen under glass. He considered a carefree smile, but then remembered he sucked at those.

At last, Alexei nodded. "Okay, we stay in. Think room service will bring us some beer?"

Mike smiled, his relief so powerful he managed a real smile. "Yeah. That would be great."

Alexei had been sure that whatever was bothering Mike would be resolved once they'd sent his father back north on his own, but he'd been wrong. There was something still there, lurking in Mike's eyes. He was trying hard to hide it, but when Alexei came out of the bathroom after his shower, he caught Mike standing at the window, looking down on the street below, with a tight, almost anguished look on his face.

Alexei put his hand on Mike's back, his skin warm through the old soft t-shirt.

Mike looked over his shoulder at him. "You remember when I first got to Moncton. How I was kind of beat up?"

"Kind of?" Alexei asked calmly, even as his stomach roiled at the memory. "Mike, you were covered in bruises."

"Right." Mike turned to look out the window again. "I told you that I'd been attacked. The night before."

"I remember." *Perfectly.*

"It happened here. In Quebec City."

Mike jumped a little when Alexei slid his hand around Mike's waist, pulling closer until his chest pressed to Mike's back and his palm rested against his belly. "I'm sorry."

He figured Mike wouldn't be comfortable with Alexei so close for long, but it was the best comfort Alexei knew how to offer. Mike surprised him when he just shuddered and leaned into Alexei's hold. "Yeah. Me, too."

Alexei didn't know what else to say. He was practically choking on the questions he'd spent most of the last four months waiting to ask. He hadn't forgotten, not for a moment, what Mike's body had looked like covered in bruises. The boot mark on his thigh.

They stood there for a long time while Mike stared out at the city and Alexei silently wished he could do something, *anything*, to make it better for Mike. The room was lit only by the lights outside and the TV flickering behind them and slowly, the intimacy broke through Alexei's rage, shifting all the adrenaline in another direction.

He carefully eased his hips away from Mike's ass, and in the process, broke the spell that had let him get away with holding Mike for a while.

Mike turned and smiled sadly. "Thanks. And sorry. You probably should have gone out with the guys. I guess I'm a drag."

Alexei just shook his head and moved to the bed. "Come. It's late," Alexei said, careful to keep his voice low as he shut off the TV. "We have an early flight."

He wondered if Mike would object to Alexei telling him it was time to go to bed, but he just nodded and crawled under the covers.

Alexei could feel Mike's heat from across the bed and ached to reach toward it. He didn't, of course, and hoped like hell he wouldn't do anything stupid in his sleep.

It had been a while since he'd been with anyone, and he hadn't missed it much or felt lonely.

Until right now.

Mike woke in the middle of the night, startled awake by his increasingly terrifying dream. For a long moment, all he could do was listen to his heart pounding and incredibly grateful he hadn't had a full-blown nightmare.

The tickle of hot breath against the back of his neck snapped him fully alert. Alexei was pressed the length of his spine, his hips snugged up against Mike's ass, a knee jammed between Mike's thighs. A wall of heat at his back.

Mike took a deep breath and Alexei's fingers twitched

against his belly where his shirt had rucked up.

The rational part of Mike's brain knew this was awkward. And not just because of his growing erection. Alexei clearly had no idea who he was using as a human body pillow. Like none. And any movement would wake him. Mike could imagine Alexei flinging himself to the other side of the bed with horror.

Which was the opposite of what the very irrational part of Mike's brain wanted.

So Mike didn't move. Not a muscle. Not to rearrange his aching dick or scratch the niggling itch along his hairline from the gusts of warm, damp breath against his skin. He just smiled and, for as long as it took for him to slip into a much better dream, enjoyed the hell out of it.

When their alarm went off at some god-awful hour in the morning, Mike smashed his face into his pillow and groaned an objection. For one glorious moment, the arm around him tightened, the weight at his back rolling on top of him as he twisted his chest against the bed.

And then it was gone.

Alexei didn't actually leap from the bed, but he didn't linger either. "I'll take the first shower," he muttered as he moved briskly to the bathroom, closing the door firmly behind him.

As a courtesy, Mike didn't point out that Alexei had just showered right before bed.

Mike popped open one eye and looked at the dawn light through the windows. It was Christmas Eve and he didn't have to go home.

Or, really, he *was* going home. To Moncton. With Alexei.

And that felt really good. Though not as good as waking up in Alexei's arms.

He gave himself permission to wallow in it for the few minutes Alexei was out of the room, turning his head and inhaling Alexei's scent from the pillow and the pocket of air beneath the rapidly cooling sheets.

The moment the shower shut off, Mike jumped from the bed and gathered his clothes for the day, crisp air and sheer will forcing his erection to subside. Alexei came out and grumbled a belated good morning, and Mike popped into the bathroom, determined to get back to business as usual.

He wasn't going to kid himself and think he could forget. What he had to remember, though, was that it just didn't matter.

Chapter Five

It took a lot of time and effort, but by early summer, the spacious one-bedroom apartment next to Alexei's was ready for occupancy. Provided, of course, that Alexei could find a tenant who didn't mind paying him under the table. Or tromping through the still-filthy warehouse. Or riding up in the freight elevator. Or the one thousand code violations in the hallway to their door.

Right.

Fortunately, there was a solution. Mike was moving in.

He already spent far more time at the warehouse than at his own apartment anyway. Before games, after practice, and the rare free day had all been spent working with Alexei on the apartment. Mike hadn't realized how lonely he'd been until he'd shared countless meals sitting on the floor or at Alexei's table. Spent hours talking while they worked, or collapsed with a beer on Alexei's big couch afterwards to review all they'd accomplished.

This place already felt like home. Moving in, at this point, was more of a formality.

"Hey, you going to stare off into space all afternoon, or are you going to lift the other half of this goddamn rug?"

Alexei's voice cut through Mike's wandering thoughts and brought him back to the dimly lit hallway. They'd just started unloading his stuff, but it wouldn't take long to finish the job. Everything he owned had easily fit in the gigantic lift.

"I still think it would have been easier to drive my car into the elevator and unload it up here."

Alexei shot him a look. "It would be easier if you picked up the other end of this rug and got to work."

Mike suppressed a smile. "Yeah, sure. Sorry about that."

He lifted his end, laughing when Alexei yanked and almost took him off his feet.

Jerk.

Muscling the thick roll through the door, Mike felt the same buzz of satisfaction he got every time he saw the results of their hard work. The polyurethane was barely dry on the hardwoods and the walls still smelled vaguely of paint, but he and Alexei had agreed the move had to be today. The post-season started tomorrow night, and for the next few weeks they would be completely focused on getting the Ice Cats to the championship.

It had been a great season, but for Mike, the best part was this. He glanced around his new living room as they unrolled the rug and squabbled over where to put it.

Not surprisingly, Alexei had a strong opinion. So did Mike.

It had taken less than a day working together for Mike to figure out that even after months of friendship, he hadn't *really* known Alexei. For starters, the easy-going prankster the team all loved was actually a bossy son of a bitch. He *loved* to argue. And when he felt passionately about something, his cheeks flushed, his eyes danced, and he threw himself into the debate.

It was sexy as hell.

Alexei listened. Argued. Laughed.

And occasionally, conceded. "Fine! You're right. The rug is better there," Alexei said, throwing up his hands.

Mike smiled.

The real Alexei was a passionate and private man. Mike would bet everyone on the team assumed the same thing Mike once had—that someone as loud and gregarious as Alexei wasn't hiding a thing—but they'd be wrong.

Alexei was quiet. Thoughtful. And brilliant. He spoke three languages fluently, a secret he had managed to keep until Mike caught him reading *Les Miserables*. In *French*. He loved to play chess, and cook, and work on his properties. He could completely eliminate his accent in the blink of an eye, negotiating with the local lumber yard like he'd been born within a ten-mile radius, then dial what Mike called his "Boris" accent up so thick, Mike could barely keep a straight face as the people around him struggled to understand a single word.

The truth was a gentle lilt that Mike would gladly listen to all day. And had.

He dropped a box against the wall next to the bookcases and stepped aside so Alexei could also set down his load.

"What have you got in here? Bricks?"

"It's all books on how to play chess."

Alexei winked on his way back into the hallway. "Too bad they don't help."

In truth, Mike was starting to hold his own against Alexei at chess, just as he did in their debates on everything from politics to hockey, and Alexei made no secret of enjoying the challenge. Hell, sometimes he brought shit up just to get the two of them going.

No, the only secret between Mike and his best friend was the one that ate at Mike every day. The one truth he knew he should have revealed before he moved in.

Mike was preparing to heft one end of his couch when his phone rang, echoing loudly in the elevator. He yanked it from his pocket and grimaced.

Home.

Why was his parents' house still labeled that?

He flashed a smile at Alexei. "Just give me a sec."

Alexei nodded, leaned one hip against the back of the couch, and crossed his arms over his broad chest.

Mike turned his back. "Hey, Mom."

"Hey, son, where are you?"

Mike sighed. It was his father. "Hi, Dad. I'm at my new apartment. I'm sure I mentioned I was moving today?"

"Shouldn't you be at the gym or on the ice? The playoffs start tomorrow."

As if Mike weren't perfectly aware of that fact. "We're not done here yet. In fact, I'm right in the middle—"

"We?" his father asked, drawing out the word. Mike cringed. *"Is it that someone special?"*

Mike looked back at Alexei and something perverse in him made him answer honestly. "Yes. It is." Then he back peddled for all he was worth. "I mean, I'm here with a friend. Look, I have to go. We—"

"Hey now. You can't just drop a hint like that and not say anything else!"

Can't I?

When Mike remained silent for too long, his father hooted, his tone absolutely gleeful. *"Tell me about her, Mike. What's her name? Where did you meet—"*

Mike did something he'd never done in his life. He hung up on his father.

Taking a deep breath, he pressed the phone to his forehead, trying to shake off the clutch of panic brought on by his father's prying. And it was his own fucking fault anyway.

Shit, he shouldn't have done that. More and more, it felt like the truth he'd kept bottled up was ready to explode out of him, and he fought it for all he was worth. And now, like a fool, he'd let one gasp escape.

Somehow that hadn't helped relieve the pressure at all. If anything, he'd made it worse.

Alexei wanted to tear the phone from Mike's white-knuckle grip and throw it down the elevator shaft. He had no idea what the hell Mike's father had said, but it had turned Mike milk-white, his dark eyes darting around the elevator as if searching for something.

"You okay?"

Mike's head snapped up. "Sure."

Alexei wondered if Mike was trying to convince Alexei or himself. Wasn't working either way. Alexei rounded the couch and stopped a few feet from Mike.

"Look, I usually follow the rule that you shouldn't say things about other people's families, but I'm going to make an exception. You always seemed stressed out when you talk to them. Can't you just...I don't know, ignore them?"

Mike stared at the wall. "They just want me to be happy."

Alexei put a hand on his arm and placed himself in Mike's line of sight. "Seems like they kind of have the opposite effect."

Mike's smile was sad. "Yeah. Well, they don't know I'm— they don't know me."

"You're a good person, Michael. A great hockey player and a hard worker. They should be proud of you."

Muscles and warm skin flexed against Alexei's fingers. Mike looked even sadder.

"Thanks," Mike said quietly.

Alexei realized he was stroking Mike's arm with his thumb and snatched his hand away. "Only the truth," he said gruffly, returning his attention to the couch.

"Alexei?"

"Yeah."

"There's something I need to talk to you about."

Alexei picked up his end of the couch experimentally. Jesus, now he remembered why he'd stuck this fucker in a storage unit.

"What's that?" he managed to grunt, eyeing Mike's empty hands.

Mike hesitated, then shook his head. "Never mind. It can wait."

Alexei would have shrugged if he weren't being crushed

under the weight of his poor furniture choices of days past. "Okay. Let me know."

He groaned as Mike lifted the other end of the couch and soon they were busy bitching about getting the thing through the door, the phone call from home, and whatever Mike had wanted to talk about, forgotten.

They threw themselves into getting Mike settled, jumping on whatever needed to be accomplished next. Once the unloading was done, Alexei unpacked Mike's kitchen, giving Mike shit about his craptastic grocery store pots and pans. Then it was the bathroom, where he stoutly refused to let his imagination wander when he chucked the large bottle of lube into a drawer. He thought about giving Mike a hard time about it, but the words got stuck in his throat.

Moving right along.

He dove into the boxes of books along the wall of built-in bookcases, trying to make sense of the chaos. Beneath stacks of sci-fi and mysteries, Alexei was delighted to find there actually *were* books on chess, as well as carpentry, plumbing, and tiling. Alexei put them into subject order on the shelves, picturing the ornate tile design Mike had created in the master bath shower.

He looked down at the next stack of books in his hands. They were all about Russia. And Moscow.

He shoved them on the shelf, his sorting system forgotten.

Next!

But the sight of Red Square haunted Alexei for the next hour. Not because he missed it—which he did, on rare occasions—but because even though the books were relatively new, the spines were cracked as though they'd been read all the way through.

Did he buy those because of me?

Alexei vacillated between being annoyed and touched.

Both of which irritated him.

He and Mike were friends. Neighbors now, which was the

best and worst idea Alexei had ever had. It had seemed simple enough when they'd first discussed it, but now it felt...*really goddamn intimate.*

If nothing else, it meant he probably should come out to Mike, a task he had put off for far too long. He didn't think Mike would freak, but people had surprised him before.

For now, though, they only had a few hours left to get Mike unpacked. Whatever they didn't finish today would have to wait weeks, until the play-offs were over. In the meantime, coming out could wait.

Mike was quiet for the rest of the afternoon, only loosening up once they stopped to have dinner and a beer in Mike's new kitchen. They had to eat standing up, of course, since Mike didn't have a table and chairs yet.

"We might have time to go shopping at the storage unit this weekend," Alexei offered.

Mike shook his head. "No way. You've already done enough."

"Are you really going to argue with me?" Alexei asked, delighted to list all the reasons he was going to win this argument. "You don't have a table. Or chairs. You won't have time to shop for weeks. *And* you always put off spending money until practically forced to at gunpoint. Hell, if I don't get you that table, you'll still be standing up to eat years from now."

"No, I won't."

"Really?"

"Of course not. I'll be over at your place, getting you to cook for me. Your chairs are probably more comfortable anyway."

Alexei took a sip of his beer to hide his smile. Damned if Mike wasn't right. Alexei's chairs were better. And he would let Mike come eat anything, anytime he wanted.

On that note, Alexei decided that it was time to go home. It had been a long day, and they had to be at the rink at the crack of dawn.

Mike said goodnight without an argument.

Alexei trudged to his apartment and crawled into bed. It was strange knowing Mike was on the other side of the wall, but rather than keep Alexei awake, he slipped into a deep sleep almost immediately.

Hours later, he woke with a jolt. The silence in his bedroom was absolute.

Then he heard an anguished cry for help.

Chapter Six

A loud crash yanked Mike out of his nightmare, his hoarse cries still searing his throat. He bolted upright in his bed.

Oh Jesus. It was just a dream. Just a dream. Just a dream.

He scrubbed his hands over his face and tried to slow his pounding heart as reality slid back into focus.

And reality was his bedroom doorknob imbedded in the brand-new wall and Alexei hovering by the bed, silhouetted in the light from the hallway.

Shit.

"What the fuck happened?" Alexei asked, searching the room for some unknown threat.

Shit. Shit. Shit. "Nothing. Christ, I'm sorry. I didn't mean to wake you."

"Wake me? What the fuck? Are you okay?"

"Yeah, I'm fine. Bad dream." Mike turned on the bedside lamp, hoping Alexei didn't see how his hand shook. He needed to chase the last of the shadows away.

Alexei searched his face. "A nightmare?"

Mike considered making up some shit, but the lie got stuck in his throat.

"Yeah," he admitted, then realized he was lying after all. "Actually, no."

"Not a nightmare?"

"It was more of a memory. Kind of a flashback, I guess."

"A flashback?"

"Yeah. I guess I should have warned you, but I really thought they were gone."

"This has happened before?"

"I'm sure it's just the new place and the play-offs fucking with my head. This is the first time I've moved since...Well, anyway, it was probably a one-time thing. I'm sorry."

"Stop apologizing."

"Okay." What else was he supposed to say? Alexei sounded really pissed, but Mike couldn't tell if it was about the apologies or having been woken up by him screaming at the top of his lungs.

"What were you remembering?" Alexei asked gently.

Mike shook his head and raked his fingers through this hair, not surprised Alexei had asked but reluctant to reveal the details. Especially since those came with that long-overdue confession.

He held himself rigid when Alexei sat beside him and laid a comforting hand on his thigh, acutely aware that he was only wearing his boxer briefs and Alexei was only in pajama bottoms. He thought he should probably move away, but since most of him wanted to burrow into Alexei's warmth and stay there, like maybe forever, holding still seemed like a decent compromise.

He couldn't help but wonder if Alexei wouldn't touch him like this if he knew the truth. That more than anything made the decision for him.

"Quebec City."

Alexei stilled beside him, presumably unaware of how hard he was suddenly gripping Mike's thigh.

"Four guys jumped me. Out of nowhere." He swallowed against the bile rising in this throat. "It's not like I haven't been in a ton of fights, but—it's different on the ice, you know? I didn't even call for help at first, just protected my face. My head. Mostly. How stupid is that? I don't even know how long it lasted. How many times they hit me before it finally clicked that no official was going to step in before it got too bad and I shouted something. Thank god someone scared them off."

He stopped to catch his breath, having spit most of the story out in a single rush. More than just the beating, not knowing how far they would have taken it had someone not heard him was what haunted Mike the most. He hated that some of the details were still hazy, that he could barely remember their faces, but he couldn't forget that two of them had been wearing hockey jerseys. That detail had always remained crystal clear.

The hand on his leg tightened, hard enough to leave bruises, but Mike was grateful. It kept him anchored in the present.

"Why would they do that? Were they trying to rob you?"

And here was the rub. "No."

"For fun?" Alexei asked with disgust.

Mike swallowed again. Hard. "They didn't like who I was with."

"I don't understand. You weren't alone?"

Mike couldn't look at Alexei, so he stared at the wall instead. "I'd just left a bar with a man I'd met that night. His name was David," he recalled, sadly. He'd been handsome. Sweet. The first man Mike had ever flirted with, overtly. With intent. It had been so fucking freeing. Mike had taken the first blows while shoving him away and telling him to run. "We—I kissed him. Right out in the middle of the sidewalk." God, it had been the bravest and stupidest thing he'd ever done.

Until possibly this moment, right now.

Alexei's hand slid from Mike's thigh and Mike's chest went painfully tight. It was hard to breathe. He told himself he'd survive this, too, no matter what happened.

"You kissed him," Alexei repeated in a monotone.

Mike looked at his best friend and wished like hell he'd done this some other way. Months ago. But all he had was now. "I'm gay."

It was the first time in his life he'd said the words out loud.

He thought Alexei would be shocked. Instead he looked...baffled. "Are you sure?"

Mike almost chuckled, but feared it would come out sounding bitter. "Pretty sure."

"But—"

"I'm sorry," Mike said quickly, suddenly certain he didn't want to hear whatever Alexei was about to say. He practically crawled over Alexei to get out of bed but didn't know where to go once he was standing beside it. What to do. Where to look. He paced in a tight circle and tried to explain. "I should have told you. Of course. I never intended to lie about it, exactly. It's just—I don't—it was the one time, really, so it hasn't really been an issue." That, he supposed, was one way to describe his complete lack of a sex life. He shook off that thought and tried to stay focused on what Alexei might actually care about. "I should have told you before I moved in. I can go—"

Mike jerked to a halt when Alexei sprang to his feet.

"Shut up."

Mike's heart constricting painfully in his chest. "I can move out after the play-offs."

"*Shut. Up.*"

Mike edged toward the door. "I'll go now."

"You will not," Alexei growled, clamping a hand around Mike's arm.

Mike pressed his back to the wall, pinned under Alexei's narrow green gaze. For the first time in months, he wished he was invisible again, even to Alexei.

It broke his fucking heart.

He'd read about coming out, tried to figure out how people did it, but it was still different than he'd expected. Scarier and easier and worse, and not helped at all by the fact he was pretty sure he'd just botched his first attempt fairly spectacularly.

Alexei couldn't decide if he was going to throttle Mike. Or kiss him.

Oh hell, who the fuck was he kidding?

Cupping the back of Mike's head in his palm, he dragged his wide-eyed friend closer and pressed his mouth to Mike's. It was an awful lot like kissing a statue.

It was way too fucking late to wonder if Mike was as certain about his sexuality as he'd claimed to be. *Hello, awkward.*

Alexei thought he should probably back away and start apologizing his ass off, but he didn't fucking want to. Not now that he'd tasted Mike's lips, felt his warm skin. He relished the feeling of Mike's full lower lip dragging against his own, greedily inhaling the scent of sleep-warmed skin and soap and sweat.

Months of telling himself he wasn't going to do this, go here, touch *anything*, made him try, but it didn't seem to matter. With a last peck to Mike's still-frozen lips, Alexei sighed, defeated, and eased his grip on Mike's neck.

Mike's quiet whimper froze Alexei in place. He hovered close. Unsure.

Then suddenly his arm were full, Mike's chest slamming into his, their mouths crashing together.

Arousal and elation seared through Alexei, all the way down to his goddamn toes. Mike whimpered again, shoving himself as close to Alexei as he could get, so that Alexei had no choice but to push back, plastering Mike against the wall.

Mike held him closer, tighter, his hands clenched around Alexei's hips. Alexei dragged his fingers up into Mike's hair. Mike's tongue slid over his, their noses bumping as they sought the best angle, took the kiss deeper. Alexei sucked Mike's tongue into his mouth, reveling in the long, low groan vibrating up from Mike's chest. Then he let it go to catch Mike's lip in his teeth and tug.

The needy sound that tore from Mike's throat make Alexei's knees weak.

He pulled back and gasped for breath, loving the bright spots of pink high on Mike's cheekbones, the trembling in his hands on Alexei's hips.

"*Moi milyy.*"

The words rumbled from him, helplessly fond and possessive and incredibly stupid. The sound of his own voice, the foolish hope packed into those two little words, snapped him out of his half-crazed stupor and plunged him back into cold reality—thirty seconds and one crazy-hot kiss *way* too late.

He stepped back, gently pushing Mike's hands away until they dropped to his sides.

"I'm sorry. I shouldn't have done that," he said quietly, backing towards the door.

"What?" Mike said, surprised. And hurt. Alexei tried to take another step, to retreat farther, but Mike latched onto his arm, stopping him. Mike looked mussed and confused and absolutely fucking adorable. Alexei pulled against his grip.

Mike wouldn't let go. "What just happened?"

"I kissed you."

"I noticed," Mike said, his shy smile like a kick to Alexei's chest.

"I'm sorry. I can't—I should go."

"No. Please." Mike grabbed his other arm. "Why are you sorry?"

"Because I shouldn't have done it.

"Then why did you?"

"I would have thought that was obvious."

"Not to me."

Alexei believed him. Mike had no idea why someone might

kiss him, let alone fantasize about it for months beforehand. When had cluelessness become so damn appealing?

"I wanted to," Alexei confessed.

"Why?"

Alexei knew the answer, just like he knew he couldn't tell Mike the truth. The reasons why it should never have happened to begin with. "Because you're hot?" he offered instead, wincing as soon as the words were out. Flirting was a really dumb deflection strategy. Jesus.

Mike smiled. "Thanks."

"You're welcome," he grumbled crossly.

"Are you gay?"

Alexei arched an eyebrow. "Are you done asking questions with exceedingly obvious answers?"

Mike laughed. "No, apparently."

Alexei felt his lips twitch. "Yes, Michael, I'm gay."

Mike seemed to think about that for a while, and Alexei watched, transfixed, as his eyes creased up, glinting with humor. "You and I really need to work on our communication."

Alexei laughed. It was so fucking true. Mike's laughter and wide grin made his chest tighten uncomfortably. He couldn't do this. Couldn't risk what he and Mike had already.

"I should go," Alexei said firmly. "We can talk in the morning." Though he really kind of hoped they didn't talk about this. Ever.

"But—"

"Good night. No more bad dreams, okay?" Which, of course, was a stupid thing to say. He sighed. "Is there anything I can do?"

"Yes."

"What?" He took an unconscious step toward Mike, willing to do whatever he could to keep his nightmares at bay.

"You can kiss me again."

Except that.

Alexei gritted his teeth, his cock twitching in spite of his sure knowledge that kissing Mike had been and would be a huge mistake.

"Mike, think about it. We're friends. Teammates. For Christ's sake, now we're *neighbors*. It would be...be a..."

Alexei's perfectly logical argument trailed off as Mike slid closer, hovering there, their lips a breath apart. Mike had a few inches on Alexei, but somehow he could look down on Alexei and plead with more eloquence than the most seductive, experienced lover Alexei had ever had kneel at his feet.

Oh, fuck it. Alexei was weak. Fallible. Only human in the face of being offered what he wanted. So. Damn. Much.

There was no hesitation from Mike this time. This kiss was all eager lips and grasping hands and, holy fuck, within seconds Alexei wanted to climb Mike like a goddamn jungle gym. Instead he poured all his frustration and need and total lack of sense and caution into kissing Mike.

Mike kissed him back like his life fucking depended on it.

Alexei shuddered, exhilarated by the desperation, the hunger, in Mike. His head spun with each needy groan rumbling up from Mike's chest. His arms ached pleasantly where Mike's fingers clenched around his biceps.

He wrapped his hands around Mike's jaw and took complete command of the kiss. Of Mike.

It was a test. A last gasp at seeing reason. Alexei might just come to his senses, force himself to walk away, if Mike was like most men and fought him for control. Pushed back against Alexei's natural inclination to dominate. Why *wouldn't* Mike do that, since he fucking loved to argue with Alexei about everything else?

But on this, they seemed to be in perfect agreement. Mike held on and whimpered and let Alexei do whatever the fuck he wanted. When Alexei bit his lip, Mike's hips arched forward, grinding his erection into Alexei's belly.

With a low growl, Alexei tore his mouth away. Mike's softly murmured protest sent chills down his spine. Goddamn, he wanted this man. And he would have him. If only just this once, he would fucking *have* him.

He stripped the sheets to the foot of the bed, shoved Mike onto his back, and knelt between his wide-spread legs. The seam of Mike's boxer briefs dug into his soft sac, his heavy erection trapped beneath dark cotton. His skin glowed, flushed from his cheeks, down his neck and across his chest.

"God, you're gorgeous like this," Alexei muttered.

Mike stared up at him, unblinking. "Look who's talking."

Alexei took in Mike's calm. His absolute acquiescence in the face of Alexei wanting to eat him alive. It burned through Alexei, as powerful as any touch or kiss could be. He bent to capture Mike's mouth, the kiss ferocious. Bordering on punishing.

Mike took it, moaning his pleasure as he lay pinned beneath Alexei. His hands clutched at Alexei's back, spine arching to bring their bodies together, their cocks rubbing through layers of cloth.

Alexei shuddered again and let the leash on his control slip, just a little, kissing Mike as he truly wanted. He nipped Mike's tongue, his lips, each bite a little harder. A little closer to drawing blood.

Mike writhed beneath him.

Alexei scored his teeth down Mike's neck, along his collarbone. He listened to Mike's groans and gasps, felt the roll of his hips, and searched, determined, for the line Mike wouldn't cross.

Damned if Alexei could find it anywhere.

Sinking his teeth into the flesh of Mike's pectoral, his tongue laved the nipple as he bit harder. Farther. Mike arched into his mouth and thrust both his hands into Alexei's hair.

"Yes. God, yes, that's good."

Now Alexei was moaning. He ground his cock against Mike's, trying to find relief, trying to understand how Mike could love this. To seem to want everything Alexei dished out as much as Alexei loved to dish it.

Alexei tortured the other nipple until it, too, stood at attention, and then bit again, his heart pounding at the thought of his mark lingering on Mike for days after. He dragged the broad flat of his tongue downward and left a shiny line over Mike's sternum, then nipped each bump of Mike's abs as he traveled lower.

Mike jerked against his mouth with every sting, begging for more. His grip in Alexei's hair was painful. Perfect.

Alexei looked up the long line of Mike's torso, expecting to see Mike's head thrown back. His eyes squeezed shut. But instead he found himself staring into Mike's wide, smoldering gaze. Mike's teeth dug into his own swollen bottom lip harder than anything Alexei had done.

He arched one brow, a jumble of thoughts and desires muddling his brain. "I don't even know where to begin."

Mike's Adam's apple bobbed, his voice hoarse when he said, "Do whatever you want."

Alexei thought he might have died and gone to fucking heaven. How long had he wanted a man to say those exact words to him? How many times had he been disappointed?

He growled against Mike's smooth, flat belly, rewarding Mike for his gift by driving his tongue into the deep divot of his navel while his teeth sank into firm muscle.

"Alexei!"

He couldn't tell if Mike meant to shout his approval, or beg him to go on. He smiled against the barely-there trail of silky hair beneath Mike's belly button, nuzzling along its length until his chin caught on the band of elastic at the waist of Mike's boxer briefs. His long, hard shaft pressed against Alexei's throat. Beseeching eyes begged him to keep going.

Alexei sat up on his heels, no longer touching Mike anywhere. Mike didn't protest. Didn't grab or squirm or make demands. He simply stared up at Alexei and waited.

Alexei felt the slow smile crawl over his face, unable to mask the unexpected joy of having Mike, willingly, happily, at his mercy. Goddamn, he was *perfect*.

Mike made a questioning noise, a little whimper accompanied by his brows quirking and his eyes darting to the bedside table. Alexei waited, watched how Mike held still, not doing anything until Alexei nodded once. Only then did Mike snake his arm out and yank open the drawer. He immediately tucked his hand back at his side.

Alexei scanned the contents of the drawer, his eyebrows steadily lifting.

Condoms. Lube. Dildos. Plugs.

"My, my, Michael, you are full of surprises."

"I only meant…" Mike's cheeks went pink.

He leaned in to examine a few of the items more closely. "A bit of a size queen, aren't you?"

Now Mike's face glowed scarlet, even the blush on his chest turning a dull red, and Alexei couldn't help but laugh.

"No, I—"

Mike's voice strangled off on an embarrassed groan when Alexei lifted the largest of the dildos from the drawer and hefted its considerable weight against his palm. "I think I'm intimidated."

"I don't—"

"Don't you?"

Mike's wide, unblinking eyes were answer enough. He most certainly did.

The only question remaining was what Alexei would do with all this new information. "Do you want me to put this in you?"

"No."

No hesitation. Mike's eyes never left his, not once straying to the huge toy in his palm or anything else in the drawer. He was utterly focused on Alexei.

Alexei sucked in a deep breath and barely resisted pressing the heel of his palm against his now-painfully erect cock.

"What *do* you want, Michael?"

"You."

Chapter Seven

Mike waited the longest, most excruciating minute of his life as Alexei considered his shameless, honest plea. Sprawled across the bed beneath Alexei's scrutinizing gaze, Mike was painfully aware of his hot blush and helpless need. Months of suppressed emotions were no doubt blatant on his face, in his eyes, and he didn't care. All that mattered was whatever Alexei did next.

"Get up, get naked, and get on your knees on the bed."

Mike was on his feet before Alexei had finished speaking. His boxer briefs were gone a second later, his face to the mattress a second after that.

This. This was what he wanted.

Alexei draped himself over Mike like a warm, living blanket. His lips brushed the shell of Mike's ear when he spoke. "I didn't tell you to bend over. I told you to kneel."

Mike immediately tried to get up, annoyed at himself for fucking up, but Alexei held him in place.

"No. Stay. I like that you did this."

Mike closed his eyes and nodded against the cool sheet as a rush of pleasure wound through him at Alexei's praise. A needy sound escaped when Alexei's weight lifted off his back.

Two hands cupped his ass, smoothing over skin and spreading him open. Exposing him completely.

"I've wanted to do this, *see* this, since the moment I realized you were waxed clean. Since that first night in the showers."

Mike's face heated again, even as blood surged into his cock and his balls snugged tighter to his body. Alexei had thought about this. About *him*. For just as fucking long as Mike had.

The happy noise erupting from Mike's chest probably ought to have been embarrassing.

One hand gently tapped his ass rhythmically. "I ought to spank you for not telling me the truth." Each touch was firmer than the one before, but they still weren't more than a pat. Mike's entire focus narrowed down to where each blow landed.

"I'm sorry," Mike gasped, afraid to ask which truth Alexei meant. That he was gay? A size queen? The happiest man alive with his face smashed to the bed and his ass in the air? There was a lot of fucking truths being revealed in this bed right then.

"Does your family know? Your father?"

A chill ran down Mike's spine, tightening every muscle. "Jesus Christ, *don't*."

Alexei's hand landed and remained pressed to his skin. "Spank you?" Challenge edged his voice.

"No, for the love of Christ, don't bring up my *father*."

Alexei chuckled. "Fair enough."

Alexei cupped Mike's balls in one hand, the other reaching forward to wrap around his cock. "So, yes to spanking?" Alexei asked curiously, casually, in the same tone he would use to confirm they'd chosen pizza for dinner.

"*Please*."

A hand pumped along the length of Mike's shaft and he groaned, as pleased with his reward as Alexei seemed to be with his answer.

"Really?" Alexei sounded distinctly dubious.

Christ, Mike didn't know how to make Alexei believe. Mike had to swallow just to get his voice to work and resorted to blurting out the unvarnished truth. "Yes. Spank me. Fuck me. Whatever you want."

Mike's head was still spinning with the sound of his own voice begging to be fucked, when his balls were released, followed by the sounds of Alexei rummaging around in his bedside drawer. Mike's heart rate doubled, his ass clenched. He squeezed his eyes shut and told himself to chill the fuck out before he blew from barely a touch.

God, but what a touch. It was *Alexei*. Alexei's hand on his dick. Alexei's firm lips brushing across the small of his back, murmuring unexpectedly sweet things. Mike had never thought of himself as sexy. Or beautiful—god, Alexei had just called him *beautiful*—until now. He felt the sting of tears in his eyes and screwed them shut tighter.

A fingertip slid down his crack and over the wildly sensitive skin surrounding his hole. Mike jerked against the teasing pressure, blindly attempting to impale himself. To get what he'd been craving for months and distract himself for everything he'd never even had the nerve to dream of hearing and having with Alexei.

The touch disappeared.

"I'm in charge, Michael."

"Yes." *Thank god.* It was what he wanted. *Needed.* And not just because he was embarrassingly inexperienced. It was bigger than that.

Cool lube circled his entrance but this time he held perfectly still. "I'm going to do what I want. That's what you said."

Mike's entire focus was honed down to the press and tickle of that one finger. He could barely get it together enough to mumble, "I meant it."

Alexei worked at the muscles surrounding his hole, pressing and massaging. Fighting tightly clenched muscles. Mike whimpered, begging for the invasion, straining to hold still and scolding himself to relax.

God, he thought he might die of happiness and relief when Alexei's thick finger finally slid into him. Easing deeper, farther. He wanted to beg him to keep going, to stretch him more, faster, but then Alexei rotated his hand, his fingertip brushing against Mike's prostate, and all he could do was groan.

"Does that feel good?"

Mike practically sobbed. "I thought we were done asking questions with exceedingly obvious answers?"

A calloused palm landed against his ass, hard, the loud crack of skin meeting skin echoing in the air around them. Fire spread from beneath Alexei's palm straight into Mike's cock, blitzing Mike's brain.

"Do you want another?" Alexei asked, his deep voice loaded with threat.

"*Yes.*"

A second finger pushed into his ass, catching Mike off guard. He yelped.

Alexei stilled.

"I thought you meant another spank," Mike gasped, his head floating somewhere above his body. He'd clenched tight when Alexei had spanked him and now Alexei's second finger felt big. Bigger than it should. Way fucking better than anything.

"Is that a complaint?"

Mike gave a breathless laugh. "No. God, no."

"Good." Mike could hear Alexei's smile.

His sweet reward was a whack to the other cheek. He clenched again, the zing heavenly. "More."

"Do we need to review who's in charge here, Michael?"

"No." Not even a little.

Mike grabbed great handfuls of his own hair in his fists, trying to ground himself as he lay still, silent, and waited. He took a deep, stuttering breath when Alexei began to pump his fingers, deep in his ass. Thrusting, then scissoring them apart.

It was too much. Not enough. *Too good.* Mike was desperately afraid he was going to embarrass himself.

Alexei's thrusts became more powerful, deeper, the

muscles loosening quickly, opening for Alexei. Pleasure unraveled, sending jolts of ecstasy to every part of Mike's body. He swore he felt each hair on his body stand at attention.

"Please, god. Hurry."

"You're not ready," Alexei said gruffly, not bothering to remind Mike he wasn't the one making the decisions. They both understood now that Mike was begging for exactly that reason.

"Yes, I am."

"I don't want to hurt you."

I do. I want you to hurt me. Just a little. Please.

Mike couldn't say it. He buried his face against the bedding and tried to breathe. Again, he lamented his utter lack of experience. Maybe lots of guys were like him? Maybe Alexei would—

Insert a third finger.

Mike lifted onto his elbows and shouted something unintelligible.

Alexei chuckled. It was the sexiest sound *ever*.

Mike spread his knees wide, his cock dragging across the bedding with every thrust, leaking pre-come on the sheet, his belly. Heat spooled in his spine, his stomach twisting with the need for the release he held back.

"Please, Alexei. *I need you*," he cried.

Alexei's hand stilled, thrust deep, and Mike hung his head between his tense shoulders, furious at his own stupidity as Alexei slowly withdrew his fingers.

Mike was ready to beg, seriously get down on his knees on the floor and *beg* Alexei to finish what he'd started, when he heard the sound of tearing foil.

He smashed his face to the mattress, his hands fisting in the sheets on either side of his head, and tried to remember to breathe.

Alexei stared down at Mike's long, lean back. His thighs spread wide across the bed. His white-knuckle grip on the sheet.

He wanted to fucking *ravage* the man.

He counted to ten, slowly.

Alexei's hands steadied enough to roll on the condom and slick his shaft with lube. He studied his red handprints on Mike's ass and almost lost sight of his intention to go gently.

"Roll over."

Mike did as he was told. Instantly. Without question.

Alexei ran his hand down Mike's chest, admiring the strength, all the more entrancing because it lay waiting quietly, for him. "*Moi milyy.*"

"Yes?" Mike couldn't possibly know what the fuck those words meant, but he apparently could intuit they were for him.

"Kiss me again."

Mike smiled. "If you insist."

Alexei *would* have insisted if he'd had to. Anything to keep his mouth busy so more crazy declarations—in any language—couldn't fall out.

Mike's tongue twined with his, his hands rubbing over Alexei's shoulders. Down his back. His legs came up to hug Alexei's ribs. Alexei hooked his elbow behind one of Mike's knee and pinned it to his chest. His other hand fisted around his own cock, desperately trying to force back the ferocity of his need while guiding the head to press against Mike.

Mike fingers scrabbling across Alexei's back as a high whine leaked from his throat. Their mouths parted on a gasp. "Yes, please, please, *please* Alexei."

Alexei's head spun, trying not to allow Mike's demands, his pleas, to distract him as he pressed forward, trying to be gentle. To go slow. It was almost impossible when every nerve in his body screamed at him to *take.*

Mike lifted his hips, twisting, pushing back. Alexei dug his fingers into Mike's thigh, trying to still him and probably only succeeding in leaving bruises, then shoved forward into unbelievable tight heat. With another push, he sank all the way to the root.

"Jesus, Michael."

"Oh god, yes. *Finally.*"

Alexei chuckled at the relieved cry until he caught Mike's gaze and the sound died. His mouth went dry.

Mike wrapped his hands around Alexei's neck, thumbs brushing his cheekbones, and pressed his lips to Alexei's. Alexei fell into the kiss, suddenly lost. Always, in the past, this was the part where his focus would hone down to one thing, one function, and the pleasure to be derived from that. From fucking.

But Mike confused the shit out of him.

Alexei's hips moved—he couldn't have stopped that if he'd tried—and Mike's rose to meet them. The groans and gasps and the dull sound of bodies bumping against one another were all the same. But the kiss didn't end. Alexei couldn't stop clutching his friend closer.

God, he was such an idiot. He was *making love* to Michael.

His strokes got longer. Deeper, dragging out the pleasure. The sounds louder, but still his mouth was sealed to Mike's. Alexei shifted and the head of his cock glanced over Mike's prostate. Mike threw back his head and sucked in a deep, desperate breath before letting it out with a howl.

"*Alexei!*"

Alexei latched onto Mike's neck. His collarbone. His shoulder. He thrust harder and faster, trying to nail that spot every time. Trying to give Mike what he needed, so that he could hear his name endlessly in increasingly desperate cries.

Alexei loved that sound. It dragged him to the edge. He'd

been close from the moment they'd started this, but now teetered on the precipice. He held on through sheer will because Mike *had* to go with him.

Mike felt like he was coming apart at the seams.

Nothing he'd done to himself had prepared him for the feeling of Alexei stretching him open. Moving inside him. Stroking his cock over Mike's sweet spot.

He bit his lip, trying not to make so much damn noise, but it was no good. He had to let it out. He wanted Alexei to know. Hell, he'd tell all of Moncton if he could.

"God, Alexei. Do it. Harder. *Please*."

Alexei's expression fierce as he reared up onto his knees and pinned Mike's knees to his chest, tilting his ass higher. "Are you sure?"

The rough timbre of Alexei's voice sent a shiver down Mike's bowed spine. "Holy shit, *are you kidding me?*"

He thought he heard Alexei chuckle, but would never be sure because the next thrust blew his fucking mind. He gasped, wondering deliriously, *joyously*, as if Alexei had literally punched the air from his lungs. The grip on his thighs was bruising, perfect, but not as mesmerizing as Alexei's face as he stared down to where their bodies were joined.

Stars burst to life in the edges of Mike's vision with every thrust. He writhed. Shouted insensible, possibly insane things when Alexei grabbed his hips and lifted him higher.

Alexei punched his hips forward again.

Mike's world went white and he bellowed Alexei's name. He shook with the strength of his climax, hot come hitting his chest and chin, his balls twisting almost painfully with each convulsion. Sore, well-used muscles clamped around Alexei's shaft, still sawing in and out of Mike's body.

It hurt so fucking *good*.

Alexei shoved as deep as he could go, sending another shock through Mike's body.

"*Michael*," Alexei whispered, followed by that word Alexei had used before.

Shudders racked Alexei and shivered through Mike as his lover, his best friend, silently came apart. Mike cupped Alexei's face, to the strong jaw that fit perfectly in his palm, and ran his thumb over a broad cheekbone.

Jesus, Alexei was beautiful. Mike wanted to watch Alexei like this for hours.

For a long time, they stayed like that, just holding on to each other and trying to remember how to breathe. It was still far too soon when Alexei's grip eased and he focused on Mike's face. His heart squeezed painfully at what he saw there.

"I'm sorry," Alexei said quietly.

Mike narrowed his eyes threateningly. "Don't you *dare*."

When Alexei opened his mouth to speak, Mike pushed himself away, groaning as Alexei's thick cock slipped from his wonderfully tender hole. *Holy crap, that's good.* Alexei grunted, temporarily too occupied with the condom to say something Mike would hate him for.

He wasn't going to let Alexei fuck this up. Not the sex. And not whatever else was between them.

"Mike," Alexei began.

Mike rolled to his feet beside the bed. His legs were decidedly unsteady. His ass felt *fantastic*.

"I'll get us something to clean us up." Mike threw the covers back onto the bed. "You stay here."

He grabbed what he needed and was gone before Alexei could say another word.

Mike was no idiot. He knew Alexei was going to try to regret this. But Mike didn't. Wouldn't. And if he never won another goddamn argument with the stupid man waiting in his bed, he would convince Alexei to give it—them—a chance.

Chapter Eight

Alexei thought he might have just done the stupidest thing he'd ever done. And that was really saying something.

Christ, it had been amazing, though.

He scrubbed his hands over his face and got out of bed, putting away the lube and straightening the bedding. He was tempted to make a run for it but that would be damn cowardly. Also, he'd never get past Mike in the hallway.

He hunted around for his pajama bottoms, searching in the sheets and under the dresser. Where the hell had they gone?

He turned to find Mike standing in the doorway, grinning. "Looking for something?"

Alexei planted his hands on his hips, almost grateful that he was too old to have recovered sufficiently to respond to Mike's blatantly thorough study.

The last thing this night needed was another erection.

"Really, Michael? You stole my pants?" Alexei took a step toward the door. "It's not like I can't just walk to my apartment like this."

Mike shrugged and leaned against the doorframe. "You can try."

"I have to go," Alexei said through gritted teeth. The thought of getting into a wrestling match was rapidly disproving his previous theory about his refractory period.

"Okay," Mike said, surprising him. "I'll come with you."

Something embarrassingly like panic clawed at Alexei. "No, you won't."

"I have a key. You going to barricade the door?"

"I might."

Mike nodded and yawned, clearly unimpressed.

Alexei suddenly recalled they had a play-off game tomorrow. Jesus Christ. Where was his head? "You need to get to sleep. You have a big day tomorrow."

"Yes, *we* do."

Alexei looked over Mike's shoulder, then at Mike, who had crossed his arms over his chest. Mike raised his eyebrows, daring him to try it.

"Fine," Alexei growled. He climbed into the bed and jerked the covers over his legs. It wasn't like he could fuck this up any more thoroughly than he already had. Jesus H. Christ, he'd just fucked *Mike*. A man who meant more to him than...well, than *anyone*. Alexei knew from experience that nothing was more likely to fuck up their friendship and force Mike from Alexei's life than trying to make them into something that couldn't possibly last.

And yet, here he was. In Mike's bed.

He glared at Mike and gestured at the empty space beside him. "Well? Let's sleep."

Mike smiled the goddamn smile he always wore when he won an argument, turned off the light, and got into bed. Alexei smashed his head into the pillow, certain he wouldn't sleep a wink. Particularly once Mike scooted closer and put his head on his shoulder. A long, heavy thigh draped across both of Alexei's and a warm hand came to rest on his belly.

Alexei's arm was going to go numb in under five minutes if they stayed like this. With a long-suffering sigh, he curled it around Mike's shoulders.

Mike said, "Goodnight," and Alexei swore he could feel Mike's smile against his chest.

"Goodnight, Michael."

Alexei woke the next morning and pulled Mike closer, burying his nose in his soft hair, soothing himself against the anxious dreams that often preceded a big game. He dozed like that for a while, half asleep, pleasantly aroused, and perfectly happy.

Then sanity returned.

Damn.

His arms hit the mattress with a thump, instantly colder for having let Mike go. He forced himself to ease from the bed, then for a long time, he stood looking down at his friend. Mike was even prettier with his dark hair going in all directions, hickeys on his neck and chest, and his long, silky eyelashes resting on his cheeks.

Damn. Damn. Damn.

Alexei practically sprinted back to his own apartment, furious when he got there and didn't know what the fuck to do with himself. He stood stark naked in the middle of his kitchen, more unsettled than he had ever been in this space.

With an irritated sigh, he stomped to his bedroom, pulled on another pair of pajama bottoms, then stormed back into the kitchen. Some music, the rising sun through the windows, and the satisfying—if unnecessarily loud—banging of pans against his stove helped restore his equilibrium.

Mostly.

He dug through the fridge and cabinets, pulled out whatever he could find, and began cooking up a storm. Blini and scrambled eggs would be perfect before a big game. He gave his entire focus to the task, not letting his mind wander to anything else.

He knew the moment Mike stepped into his apartment, but he didn't turn around.

"Good morning," Mike said from directly behind him.

He barely suppressed his startled jerk. And the desire to rip whatever clothes Mike had on, back off. Then again, maybe Mike was still naked. Alexei refused to look. "Morning."

Mike peered over his shoulder. "What's for breakfast?"

Alexei looked down at the feast he was preparing. For two. "Just what I could make with what was in the house," he said, reaching for his coffee to soothe his hoarse voice.

Mike slid around to rest one hip against the counter beside him. "Looks delicious."

Alexei made the catastrophic error of glancing at Mike. Mike wasn't looking at the food.

When Mike opened his mouth again—no doubt to say something else Alexei didn't want to hear—Alexei grabbed a plum from the fruit bowl and shoved it between Mike's lips. He ignored the bright laughter in his friend's eyes and the disappointment he felt at discovering Mike was, indeed, wearing something from the waist down.

"Eat," he said, pointing at Mike's chair at the table.

Mike went without protest, munching on the plum. Alexei tried not to stare at the flex of his jaw, the shine of juice on his lips, or the long line of his neck when he swallowed.

He imagined Mike swallowing something else entirely.

One of the blini hit the counter and bounced onto the floor.

"You all right over there?" Mike asked.

"Fine."

"Alexei, we should—"

"Shut up. I'm thinking."

Which was a patent lie, since he couldn't hold onto a thought for longer than a second.

Just the headspace a goalie should be in before a big game.

He slid the last of the blini onto their plates, scooped out eggs, and brought the food to the table. Mike took his plate without a word, and, for the first time all morning, didn't look so goddamn pleased with himself.

Alexei sat and shoveled breakfast into his mouth, preventing any conversation.

He knew damn well he was going to run out of food before

he figured out a good way to explain to Mike why this couldn't work.

Alexei was painfully aware that what he wanted, what he *really* wanted, he couldn't have. Not for the long term. And rather than settle, he'd resigned himself to being alone.

He wasn't signing up to be a monk, of course, but the men he wanted just didn't stick around for long. As far as he could tell, they didn't mind putting up with his bullshit for a while, letting him be in charge, maybe even enjoyed the novelty of being dominated, but then it was done and they were gone. There'd only been one man, once, who he'd thought might go the distance.

Turned out the only distance they'd gone was the roughly three hundred miles of Canadian countryside that now separated them.

Alexei couldn't stand the idea of losing Mike. Which was stupid, since they were teammates. Coworkers, who, with almost no warning, could be traded to another town. Province. *Country.* That alone should be reason enough to avoid a relationship. Maybe even the reason he could give Mike to avoid explaining all the other shit. Then they could move on and Alexei could think back on last night as a means for getting his desire for Mike out of his system.

Alexei almost choked on that lie, and his eggs, when Mike innocently sucked a dot of jam from his finger.

But it didn't change the truth. Alexei wanted what was best for them both. He wanted Mike's friendship. And Mike deserved a man who would make love to him every night, the way Alexei had last night. It had been good. Great. Beautiful, even. But Alexei wasn't that guy. He'd kept his promise to himself and held back. Way back. Those spanks had been nothing compared to what he'd wanted to do.

Like bite the tender skin where the curve of Mike's perfect ass met his thigh. If Alexei closed his eyes, he could imagine the bruise. The arc of his teeth imprinted on pale skin and over hard muscle. He could imagine Mike's butt glowing pink, not just with two handprints, but warmed to a rosy red all over, hot to the touch. He could almost hear the noises Mike would make when Alexei fucked him, his hips slamming into all that tender flesh.

The sound of Mike clearing his throat yanked Alexei from his wayward daydream. He snapped his eyes open and realized he'd been sitting there in la-la land, smiling like a fucking idiot.

Mike's grin had returned. He caught Alexei's glare and did a miserable job at trying to appear serious.

Alexei dropped his forehead into his palm and watched Mike from the corner of his eye as he stood, cleared his empty plate, and tackled the dishes. Watched the flex of muscle in Mike's back as he lifted a heavy pan or bent over the dishwasher. By the time Mike returned to the table, Alexei was coiled tighter than a goddamn spring, ready to hurl himself from his chair at the least provocation.

God, when had he become such a fucking wimp? *Just tell the guy it won't work, then figure out how much damage you've already done to your friendship.*

It was that last part that really had him worried. Made his breakfast turn to lead in his belly.

Mike came around the table, too close, and leaned down until their cheeks brushed, his lips tickling Alexei's ear when he whispered, "Thank you for being my first."

Alexei's heart stopped, his fork clattering down onto his plate. He looked up at Mike. "What?"

Mike smiled. "I'm going to go get ready to head over to the arena," he said evenly, as if he hadn't just dropped a bomb on Alexei. He ran a finger over Alexei's stubbly cheek. "Don't forget to shave. It's our last chance before the play-off beards start."

Alexei nodded automatically, his brain still stuttering.

He'd taken Mike's virginity last night? But the dildos...the plugs. He'd never once thought those were all Mike had ever...

Alexei sat with his mouth hanging open and watched Mike's perfect ass walk out the door.

How, in the name of all that was holy, was he supposed to play hockey when his best friend kept turning him inside fucking out?

The atmosphere in the locker room after the game that night was jubilant, the team rejoicing in having begun the play-offs with a solid win against a tough opponent.

Mike hardly batted an eye when Alexei agreed to meet everyone at Smitty's to celebrate, though he couldn't suppress an inward pang of disappointment. Alexei even managed to load a couple more guys in the truck, ensuring Mike didn't have an opportunity to suggest, let alone actually start, anything.

He'd been hoping—all damn day—that they'd do something *else* after the game. Like get naked and...

Well, hell, he wasn't even sure what they'd do after that. And he didn't care so much, as long as it was with Alexei.

And there was that naked part.

He had this vague idea that Alexei had been holding back last night. God knew, Mike was a total newb when it came to sex, but he didn't want to be coddled. Far from it. His fantasies had always been more...well, more than what anyone would consider vanilla. He had loved it when Alexei had bitten his chest. His stomach. Hell, goosebumps rose across his neck and arms just *thinking* about it. He wondered how he could coax Alexei into doing more—

He nearly jumped out of his damn skin when a heavy arm slung around his shoulder and shook him. "Earth to Mike! Come in, Mike!"

Mike laughed and looked at Garrick. "Sorry. Were you saying something?"

"Yeah, for about the last five minutes, all the while

wondering when you were going to stop staring off into space and notice I was describing, in detail, all the ways to castrate a calf."

Mike winced. "Why the hell were you talking about that?"

"To see if you were listening! Everyone else within earshot ran away."

Mike smiled sheepishly. "Sorry. Just thinking about stuff."

"Anything you want to talk about?"

No. Hell no. And no fucking way. "That's all right. I'm cool." He happened to look at the bar and saw Alexei watching them, his eyes narrowed. Mike ducked out from under Garrick's arm.

"You sure you're okay?" Garrick tracked his gaze to the bar. "Ah, now I see."

Mike's heart stopped. "What?"

"Is it the brunette? Or the blonde?"

Definitely the brunet, but not the one you're thinking of. Mike laughed nervously. "Neither."

"You sure? Because I know Sandy and Becca. I'd be happy to introduce you."

"No, really. I'm good."

Garrick sent him a speculative look. "You know, the ladies love this shy thing you have going. You probably haven't even noticed that half the regulars at these things are trailing after you most of the night. They'd probably faint if you actually smiled at one of them."

Please god, don't let that be true. "Really?" Mike croaked.

Garrick laughed, a huge guffaw that turned more heads in their direction, before leaning in close. "Dude, if I didn't know better, I'd wonder about you."

Mike choked on his beer while Garrick cracked up, whacking him on the back a few times. By the time he'd regained the ability to breathe, Garrick had wandered off.

A hand brushed down his arm. "You okay?"

He looked up, instantly soothed by Alexei's presence. "Yeah. Garrick just—" Mike almost couldn't finish the damn sentence, his chest was still so tight from the shock. "He said he wondered about me."

Alexei cocked his head. "So?"

"What if he's serious?" Mike whispered. He told himself to be chill. Garrick didn't know shit, and maybe it wouldn't be such a big deal if he did. But Mike had only come out for the first time *yesterday,* and he still could hardly believe he'd done that—though it was safe to say the reward had been far sweeter than he could ever have dreamed.

And either way, who knew and who didn't wasn't a choice he wanted to have taken away from him.

Alexei plucked Mike's beer from his hand and put it on the table beside them, startling Mike out of his spiraling thoughts. "Come on. We're going home."

Mike didn't argue, grabbing his coat and saying goodnight to everyone as he followed Alexei out onto the street. They'd parked Alexei's truck at home and walked the few blocks to the bar.

Now it was later. And colder. Mike forced himself to leave a respectable distance between himself and Alexei, even though there was no one out on a night like tonight.

Jesus, one minute he was freaking out about being outed, the next he wanted to hold Alexei's hand on the street. This shit was stressing him out.

"Stop it."

He looked at Alexei. "What?"

"You're thinking so hard I can practically smell the smoke coming from your ears."

"I guess I'm worried about what Garrick said. What if he thinks I'm gay?"

"Dude, you *are* gay, remember?" Alexei said with a laugh.

"Yeah, but I play hockey."

"What the fuck is that supposed to mean? Some hockey players are gay. Some are straight. You, of all people, shouldn't be surprised by this."

"I guess I thought I was a freak." As soon as the words left his mouth, he realized how they sounded. "No, I mean—"

Alexei shoved open the side door into the warehouse and dragged Mike inside.

"Is that what you think? That you're a freak?" he demanded.

"No, of course not. "

Alexei opened the lift doors, casting a dim light across them both, then grabbed Mike's arms. "Am I a freak, Mike?" he asked, far more gently.

"No."

Alexei was amazing. Smart. Funny. Loyal. Kind.

And yeah, rightfully annoyed with Mike if the way he sighed and scrubbed his hands over his face was any indication.

"There are plenty of gay guys in the sport," Alexei said reasonably. "Just look at Garrick."

Mike blinked. "What? You're joking, right? He dates, like, *tons* of women."

Alexei snorted. "And if I catch him staring at your ass one more time, I'm going to punch him in the face."

Mike swayed a little. God help him, he was getting an erection.

"Do you believe me?" Alexei asked gently.

"That you'd punch Garrick in the face?"

Alexei smiled. "No. That there are more than just two gay men in the whole hockey universe."

"But no one is out," Mike said.

"No, no one is out," Alexei conceded with a sad smile. "At least, not to the public or the leagues, as far as I know. But that doesn't mean their friends don't know. That they aren't in relationships. Committed and otherwise."

Mike wanted that. To be in a committed relationship.

And not just with some imagined man he might meet one day, he realized with a start.

He wanted that with *Alexei*.

He had the good sense to keep that to himself. Following Alexei into the lift, he ran through the Wild Cats roster in his head and tried to guess if anyone else on their team was gay. Then he looked at Alexei and realized he was the last one who would be able to tell. He hadn't figured it out about his own best friend.

"Why are you smiling?" Alexei asked.

"Just wishing I had much better gaydar. Mine obviously sucks and now I'm curious."

Alexei turned his back, but Mike could still see his furious scowl. "You looking for someone to hook up with?"

Mike smirked at the back of his stubborn friend's head. "No. I've got my hands full already."

Chapter Nine

As soon as the lift shuddered to a stop, Alexei devoted undue attention to getting the doors open, then strode down the hallway to his door. He wasn't surprised that Mike followed him, he just didn't know what he was going to do about. He pressed his forehead to the cool steel.

"Go home, Mike."

Mike jerked back a step and Alexei knew he didn't want to see the expression on his friend's face. That was why he made himself look.

It fucking killed him.

His every instinct screamed that he needed to do whatever it took to erase the sadness in those eyes. But he held firm.

Barely.

"We have another game tomorrow and didn't get a lot of sleep last night. We can talk about this more later." *You know, just as soon as I figure out what the fuck else I can say to convince you it's a bad idea.*

"Did I do something to piss you off?"

"No, you didn't. It's not that." Alexei dropped his bag and leaned back against his door. "Look, Mike, I'm not good at talking about shit like this," he began, leading with the understatement of the century, "but I don't think it's a good idea for us to...do that again. I don't want to fuck up our friendship."

"You say that like it's a forgone conclusion."

"Isn't it? Before last night you'd never been with anybody. You're just figuring shit out."

"But—"

"Go out. Find a nice man. Find a couple of nice men." Just

saying the words made Alexei feel sick to his stomach.

Mike didn't look much better. His barely whispered "What?" tore at Alexei.

"Mike, you don't know what you want. Who you want. Just because I was here, at the right time and the right place, doesn't mean we're good together." The words felt like a lie, but Alexei didn't back down.

"But—"

"Just think about it, okay?

"Okay," Mike agreed. He sounded like Alexei had just kicked his puppy.

"Okay, then. Goodnight," Alexei said quietly, then slipped through his door and shut it resolutely behind him.

Mike flinched at the sound of Alexei's deadbolt echoing in the hallway.

Wow, that sucked. Being told to go out and find other men was bad enough, but it was more than that. Mike *knew* Alexei. And while he had no idea what was driving Alexei to push him away, he could see that Alexei was scared.

Of him.

He turned away and walked calmly into his own apartment, not giving into the urge to slam his door with frustration or go back and beat Alexei's down to demand answers.

It was late and he knew he should go to bed, but now he was restless. Unable to settle. He paced around his apartment, cursing his lack of seating in the kitchen, before deciding it wouldn't have mattered. He didn't last five minutes on the couch. Springing up, he went to the living room bookcases and ran a hand over the books.

He was going to need a strategy. A good one. Alexei was nothing if not stubborn, and while Mike was perfectly happy to let him lead the way in the bedroom, there was no way in hell it was going to work that way outside of it.

Mike *would* win this argument.

He just had to figure out how.

An hour later, long past the time he should have gone to sleep, he was sitting on the floor in his bedroom amidst neatly folded piles of clothes waiting to be tucked back into the dresser. He'd already rearranged his hastily unpacked linen closet.

He froze when he heard a key in his door, his brain's endless churning finally grinding to a halt.

Alexei appeared in his bedroom doorway, his hands on his hips.

"What are you doing?"

Mike looked around him. "Vacuuming," he said with a straight face.

Alexei's frown deepened. Mike relented.

"I'm sorry if I woke you. I didn't think I was making that much noise."

"I couldn't sleep," Alexei confessed gruffly.

Mike stood and put down the stack of clothes he'd been holding. He knew the moment Alexei noticed he was naked.

Alexei focused on his face again. "You need to get some sleep. We have early practice."

"Okay."

Had Alexei really come over here to tuck him in?

No. He hadn't.

Mike moved slowly, as if afraid he might startle a wild animal into running away, and turned off the bright overhead light. The bedside lamp cast warm shadows over them.

Now what?

"You want to get some sleep?" he asked casually, as if this

was completely normal for them.

Alexei nodded once, then he was there, pushing Mike toward the bed. He'd barely dropped onto the mattress before Alexei slid under the covers behind him, all around him, Mike's bare ass tucked against soft flannel, Alexei's chest warming his back.

Mike snapped off the bedside light and grinned.

Mike's alarm went off at some god-awful hour in the morning, making it through four bars of some screechy pop song before Mike slammed his hand on snooze bar, and went right back to sleep.

Alexei buried his face against the back of Mike's neck and tried to do the same.

He'd slept like a baby once he'd finally given in and come to Mike last night. He'd been listening to the dull thuds coming through the wall from Mike's bedroom, wide awake, staring at the ceiling, until his curiosity had pulled him from his bed.

And landed him in Mike's.

Because he was a complete fucking idiot with zero willpower, apparently.

Alexei shifted, trying to ease his dick away from Mike's delectable ass. That he'd not sprung a woody the minute he'd curled himself around Mike last night was proof enough that he'd been exhausted.

Now, fully rested, he wasn't nearly so lucky.

As if Mike had heard his thoughts, he rolled onto his back, a little smile on his lips and a tent above his hips.

Alexei's mouth watered. He peeled the sheet away to see the long, thick length of Mike's erection standing proud.

Alexei looked up at Mike, his heart doing something funny when he found his friend smiling at him with sleep-clouded eyes and sheet marks on his cheeks. He'd never looked better to Alexei.

Though the smile was a bit too smug for Alexei's liking. He could fix that easily enough.

He took Mike's cock deep into his mouth, down his throat, then pulled off again with a huge upward suck.

"Holy fuck!" Mike shouted, his hips coming off the bed.

Alexei smiled as he rolled over Mike's legs and pinned his hips with his hands. A hundred commands sprang to mind, but he didn't bother with any of them. Mike didn't fight his hold. Didn't grab his head. Didn't do anything but stare at him with very un-smug wonder.

Alexei took him deep again, his tongue working along the shaft on the way down, his cheeks hollowing as he pulled back off. He wrapped his fingers around the silky shaft and tugged, his lips and hand bumping.

Mike curled his fists into the sheets and held on. God, he was so fucking perfect.

Why couldn't this work?

Alexei shut his eyes and his mind to the impossible question, knowing he could find countless answers if he tried, and not wanting any of them at this moment. Instead he focused on Mike, on his taste and texture, on the sounds tearing from his chest and the twitches and shivers Alexei pulled, so easily, so beautifully, from him.

The vein along the bottom of Mike's shaft throbbed against Alexei's tongue and he knew Mike wouldn't last long. Alexei reached down and wrapped a hand around his own cock, pumping furiously, bringing himself to the brink as he dragged Mike there with him.

Shudders racked Mike, his mouth gone slack, his breathing hectic as his shaft swelled against Alexei's tongue.

Alexei pulled off and ran his tight fist over Mike's cock in time with his own while crawling up the bed quickly.

Mike sucked in a huge gasp and let it out with a roar.

That did it.

Lightning shot through Alexei as his climax jolted through him. He was barely able to keep working his hand over Mike's cock as their come mixed, hot against his fingers as it slid down Mike's shaft and over his balls.

Mike whispered his name with a breathless gasp, his eyes fixed on Alexei's hands as yet more shudders shook them both.

Alexei knew it was wrong. That he shouldn't have done this. He should have been consumed by guilt. And regret.

So why the hell did he feel so fucking *content?*

Mike went into the corner full tilt and slammed Erik Larsson into the boards. He kept his shoulder down, his stick out of the way, and played within the rules while still attempting to break the son of a bitch in two.

The crowd roared their approval, their ire having escalated right alongside Mike's each time Larsson "accidentally" crashed the net. Twice already tonight.

Players didn't target goalies. It wasn't done. Particularly when that player used to be on the same team with the goalie. *This* team, in *this* town. But Larsson seemed to be making an exception tonight, and Mike wasn't going to tolerate it.

Neither were the fans. The officials, on the other hand, seemed not to care at all.

Increasingly outraged and outrageous howls issued from the stands and the bench, but Mike stayed focused on the game, on his job. Shift over, he climbed over the boards and kept his eyes pinned to Alexei. When Larsson dove for the puck and swept Alexei's legs right out from under him, *again*, Mike jumped to his feet. Only Garrick's grip on his arm kept him from charging onto the ice—and being ejected from the game—while Alexei and Larsson exchanged a few words and shoves.

What the fuck was with this guy?

Mike soared over the boards for his next shift, picking up the puck and driving it forward. His pass went wide and he drew back, blocking the next shot on goal with his body before sweeping aside the rebound.

His worked his ass off in front of the net, trying to make Alexei's job easier and jostling with whoever was at his back. Alexei made a great save and the whistle blew. Mike turned to find himself face-to-face with Larsson.

He bumped his chest into Larsson's. "Back the fuck off, asshole."

Larsson shoved him away but held onto his jersey—universal hockey language for "now we're gonna fight."

Yee haw.

Mike grinned, his blood surging in a way that no game-time fight had ever done before. Who knew sex would charge him up like this? He wanted to pound this fucker into the ice, then go home and have Alexei pound his ass into the bed.

In fact, Mike thought that just might be his version of a perfect night.

Before either of them could do more than cock back an arm, Alexei and the refs got in the way. Mike tried to get a word in with Alexei, but he was too busy glaring at Larsson.

Mike wanted to wipe the smirk off that asshole's face with his fist.

It wasn't until the third period, while Mike was fighting for a puck in front of the net, that Larsson finally sent him over the edge. Larsson crashed into him and they both flew back into Alexei, sending all three of them and the net back to the boards. His legs still tangled with Larsson's and Alexei's pads, Mike shook off his gloves and prepared to do what he'd been dying to do for hours.

Punch the fucking jerk right in the face.

Larsson sneered at Alexei. "This your new boyfriend?"

Rage burning in his gut, Mike tackled Larsson, landing on

top of him. He grabbed two fistfuls of his jersey, and yanked the douchebag's shoulders up off the ice, until their helmets cracked together. He could feel Alexei's restraining grip on his jersey, but he didn't give a fuck. No one else was close enough to hear him.

He snarled at Larsson. "You bet I am."

Mike got to enjoy the stunned look on Larsson's face for all of three seconds before a black and white striped arm hooked around his torso and hauled him away.

Time in the penalty box did nothing to soothe his temper *or* his libido.

Getting a world-class cold shoulder from Alexei in the locker room after they'd won the game didn't either.

Mike threw on his street clothes and tore out of the arena, hot on Alexei's heels. They'd come in together this morning—as usual—and he didn't *think* Alexei would strand him here, but he wasn't going to take any chances.

Alexei's furious expression made him wonder if he wouldn't be better off in a taxi anyway.

No. He wasn't going to let Alexei shut them down before they'd even had a chance to get started. That meant riding this out.

He climbed into the passenger seat and glared at his friend. "You want to tell me what crawled up your butt and died?"

Alexei's scowl got blacker and he slammed his foot on the gas so hard, Mike's head bounced off the headrest. He spent the first half of their high-velocity drive home trying to keep his ass in his seat long enough to get his seatbelt on.

Clearly, he needed to rethink his strategy. Maybe he should try a more diplomatic approach? He glanced at Alexei, skipping over his fierce frown and letting his eyes wander south.

Maybe he should offer to give Alexei a blow job? He'd never done that before, but after his experience this morning, he was eager to try it.

And it would cheer Alexei up, right?

His smile must have been as wicked as his thoughts, because Alexei appeared downright alarmed after glancing over at Mike. He drove faster, barely letting the warehouse doors open wide enough to admit the truck before he squealed into their makeshift garage.

Mike hadn't released his seatbelt before Alexei flew out of the truck and slammed the door behind him.

Mike sighed and chased after him. "Will you slow the fuck down and tell me what's wrong?"

Alexei stepped into the elevator and yanked down the door. Mike dove in after him.

"Jesus, Alexei. You almost took my head off. What the fuck is your problem?"

"You!" Alexei barked. "You're my fucking problem."

Mike swallowed and reminded himself he'd been expecting it. Sort of. It still didn't feel very good. And the mixed signals, back-and-forth shit was killing him.

"I'm sorry you feel that way," he said honestly.

Alexei seemed to deflate. "No, I'm sorry." Alexei rubbed a hand over his shoulder and Mike realized he'd been doing it off and on since they'd left the ice.

"Did that asshole Larsson hurt you?"

Alexei's hand dropped. "It's fine. Just a bruise."

Mike resisted the urge to tug aside Alexei's collar to look for himself. He watched Alexei as he lifted the massive door to reveal their hallway. He didn't see any signs of pain.

"Why was that guy all over you?"

Alexei stepped into the hallway. "He's my ex."

Mike's brain stuttered. "What?"

"Stupid fucker ended it years ago, then tried to come back a few months ago and I said no. At our last game he actually tried to flirt with me *on the ice*, and I made it very clear what I thought of that shit. Guess he's not too happy about it."

"Wait. How long did you two date?" Mike asked while he dogged Alexei's heels to his apartment door.

Alexei stopped and Mike was alarmed to see his shoulders slump. "Almost two years."

Another brain stutter. "Two years?" Shit, why was his voice so high?

"Yeah."

"What happened?" Mike asked with a mix of curiosity and dread.

"He got traded."

"So?"

Alexei stopped looking at something over Mike's shoulder and met his eyes. "He figured that meant it was over."

And you didn't.

"Did you love him?" Mike asked quietly.

"I thought it was going that way," Alexei answered, and for a moment his eyes narrowed on Mike before he looked away again. "Turns out it wasn't."

Two years seemed like an awful long time to Mike for two people to still be thinking about being in love. Mike had only had sex with Alexei two days ago, and already he was—well, he was feeling pretty strongly about the guy.

But he supposed the different timetables didn't really matter. What mattered was that Larsson had hurt Alexei. Mike regretted, more than ever, not knocking out a few of the bastard's teeth.

"I'm sorry," he said.

"For what?"

"That he ended up being an asshole."

"Eh. In hindsight I can admit he kind of started that way, too."

"I'm also sorry he convinced you that dating another player was a bad idea."

Alexei sighed. "Actually, I knew that before I dated Erik. He just added more proof."

"I wouldn't leave."

"What?"

"If I was dating someone, if I loved him, I wouldn't end the relationship just because I got traded away."

Alexei's expression stayed perfectly neutral. "Good to know."

"Yeah, well, I just thought I'd mention it." *And, you know, way overplay my hand.*

Time to change the subject. Though he did have one more related question.

"Do you have a lot of exes?" he asked as casually as he could manage. It wasn't easy when he was still plotting when he could go out and run over Larsson with his fucking car.

No, better, he'd take Alexei's truck—

Alexei smirked and turned to unlock his door. "A few."

"And they're all men?" Because he was starting to think he'd need a reinforced bumper.

"Did Erik Larsson look like a girl to you?"

Mike smiled. "You really want me to answer that? I wouldn't want to insult your taste in men."

Alexei rolled his eyes and threw open his door. Mike could have sworn he heard him mutter "you're one to talk" under his breath.

Chapter Ten

Alexei chucked his bag in the corner and made a beeline for the fridge. He needed a fucking beer.

Mike was killing him. Every time Alexei had turned around today, there Mike was. And no, that wasn't actually different than any other day, but today it was making Alexei crazy. And it was his own damn fault. What the fuck had he been thinking last night when he'd crawled into bed with Mike? Never mind this morning when he'd blown the guy.

And now he'd told him about Erik, of all things.

Jesus, he had no self-control around this man.

Like, right now he should send Mike back to his apartment, banish him from sight, but Alexei didn't bother. He was afraid he'd only go looking for Mike in the end.

He spun to give Mike a beer and found him standing six inches away.

"Back off!" he barked.

Mike immediately stepped back.

Alexei sighed. *What the fuck am I doing?*

"Look, Mike, this morning…the other night. It was nice."

Mike made a face.

"Ok, fine, it was fucking fantastic. But it can't happen again."

"Why not? What part of *fucking fantastic* isn't working for you?"

Alexei slammed his beer down on the counter. "You don't understand. I'm not like you."

"What does that mean?"

Shit. He really didn't want to have to explain this. "Just trust me. I've been around the block. A few times. You were a

99

virgin the day before yesterday."

"I never should have told you that," Mike muttered.

He grabbed Mike's arms and yanked him in close. "I'm glad you did, because—because otherwise—" *Otherwise, I might have been able to ignore all the obvious signs that we are not compatible. Because god, look at those lips. Right there. So close.* He shoved Mike away and took a step back. "You need to find a nice man who can make love to you the way you want."

"And what the hell would you know about that?"

"Will you just trust me?"

"I'd trust you with my life," he said looking Alexei right in the eyes, his gaze glinting with the determination he brought to all of their arguments. "But I'm not going to let this go."

Alexei gritted his teeth. "That's just it, Michael. You like to argue with me. Debate *everything*. And that doesn't work for me. Not in bed."

It would eventually be, Alexei was sure, the goddamn deal-breaker.

So why the hell was Mike suddenly kissing him? And why the hell was Alexei kissing Mike back?

God, Mike's tongue. Lips. His taste. Alexei could kiss him like this all night.

With a frustrated growl, he shoved Mike away again. "Did you not *hear* me?"

"I heard you fine," Mike said quietly, calm in the face of Alexei's anger.

"Then why did you kiss me?"

Mike looked at him, into him, from where he slouched against the fridge. His hands pressed to the stainless steel. Cheeks pink, chin tucked, a little smile playing on his lips. Goddamn, he got under Alexei's skin like someone had given him the operator's manual.

"Because I knew you wouldn't kiss me."

Alexei gulped. "You have no idea what you're asking for."

Mike gripped the front of his shirt and towed him closer. "Show me."

Alexei sighed and pressed his forehead to Mike's.

"Alexei—"

"No, I'll hurt you. I won't be able to resist. I can't...I can't *not* hurt you," he confessed, almost wishing it wasn't true. To be with this man...But no, Alexei couldn't change who he was any more than he would force Mike to do things he wasn't comfortable doing.

Mike leaned back and cocked his head. "Like, whips and chains and stuff?"

"No, none of that shit. Just...*rough.*"

"Tell me what you mean."

At long fucking last, Mike looked serious. Almost wary.

Dancing around the truth hadn't worked, so Alexei went with brutal honesty. "I like to be in charge. I want you do what I say, as soon as I say it. I want you to feel me—my hands, my teeth—for *days* afterward. To know your ass is sore from my cock and glowing red from the palm of my hand. I want you to wince when you sit, and then think of me. Do you understand?" He looked down Mike's long, lean body and took a deep, shuddering breath. "I could not possibly touch you again and not bite your perfect ass. *Hard.*"

Alexei watched Mike's face, waiting for the distaste, maybe outright disgust, to show. His breath caught in his throat when Mike's lips curved in a slow smile.

Mike wanted to laugh. Hell, he wanted to jump up and down and whoop and then tackle Alexei to the floor and beg him to have his way with Mike. Instead, he smothered his grin—while still not being able to completely mask his smile— and watched the mixture of frustration and determination on Alexei's face turn into panic.

It didn't take a genius to figure that Alexei had believed Mike would run screaming when he told him the truth.

That wasn't going to happen. Not when Mike wanted exactly what Alexei wanted. Jesus, Mike was *so fucking lucky.* Maybe this was some attempt by the universe to restore balance, a little slice of karmic payback for the shit in Quebec City.

Whatever it was, there was only one answer. One thing Mike needed to say.

"Yes."

Alexei blinked. "Yes, what?"

"Yes, please?"

"You can't mean—"

"That's exactly what I mean."

Alexei shook his head, scowling. "No."

"Yes. And not because it's what you want," Mike said quickly. Honestly. He ran his thumb over Alexei's cheekbone and wrapped his hand around his jaw. Because he could. And because he didn't want Alexei to run away. "I'm not saying yes because I think that's what you want to hear." In fact, it was fairly obvious the opposite was true, though Mike still couldn't quite figure out why. "I want this for me. This is what I've always wanted. It's just beautiful fucking kismet that what you just said, the things you want to do, I want you to do that. To me."

"Mike, you *love* to argue with me. You're arguing with me right now."

Mike smiled. "I do. I am."

Alexei rolled his eyes.

Mike slid his hand down Alexei's neck and chest, feeling a thrill of power when he cupped Alexei's erection in his palm. "And you like it."

"Not in bed, I won't."

"Not in bed," Mike agreed, a shiver working down his spine. "I promise, it never even crossed my mind to argue with you then."

"You were upset. I took advantage of that, and I didn't realize you'd never—"

Mike stroked his hand over Alexei's cock again, harder. "You didn't take advantage of me."

"I did. That was too rough for your first time. I should have—"

"I wanted it rougher."

"You did?" Alexei sounded genuinely bewildered. Mike almost felt sorry for him.

"I did."

"You can't know what you really want."

Mike fought the urge to grind his teeth. "I'm not a child. I know what I want. What I like."

"But you haven't been with anyone."

"I've been with you," Mike reminded him, watching how the flush on Alexei's cheeks deepened. It was hard not to be distracted by that. By the still-solid erection beneath his palm, proving that Alexei didn't mind Mike arguing with him sometimes. A lot of the time. "Let me ask you something. Your first time. Did you just lie there? Did you let him take charge?"

"No, I—" Alexei frowned harder. "That's not the point."

It was exactly the point. "I've never done a lot of things. Anything, really, that I couldn't do to myself. But that doesn't mean I haven't thought about it. What it would be like. How I'd like it to be done or do it."

He let Alexei think about that for a long moment, trying very hard not to smile at how Alexei's hands fisted in Mike's shirt, effectively pinning him to the refrigerator.

"I've never given a blow job, for example," Mike continued innocently as he ran his palm back and forth the length of

Alexei's shaft.

Alexei's pink cheeks went red. "Is that so?"

"But I know I'd like to. Give a blow job, I mean. I don't have to have experience to know that would really...do it for me."

Alexei just stared at him, green irises glowing around pinprick pupils. Mouth hanging open. It took a nice, satisfyingly long time for Alexei's eyes to regain focus and narrow on his face. "What are you waiting for, then?"

"For you. The man in charge."

Suddenly Mike was pinned to the refrigerator. His pulse leapt, working double-time to pump blood into his cock.

He didn't fight Alexei's restraint. He fucking *relished* it. Was mesmerized by the fierce need etched into every line of Alexei's face.

"Suck. My. Cock."

Alexei released him and Mike was on his knees, both hands in Alexei's waistband before Alexei had even managed to take a step away.

The determination he'd channeled into winning his argument deserted him, replaced with a desperation that made his hands shake, his whole body shiver as he fumbled with the button at Alexei's waist and peeled the fly open. Coordination shot, he clumsily shoved jeans and underwear out of his fucking way.

Alexei's rigid erection hit him in the face and he dove on it with a desperate whimper, dignity be damned. He wanted the taste of Alexei's sweat and skin on his lips. The heavy weight of Alexei's thick shaft on his tongue. Musk filled his nose, the scent stronger, richer, *sharper* than he'd dreamed.

He sucked in as much air as he could before he lunged down. And choked.

He backed off quickly, fighting the need to gag and the rude noises spilling from his throat. He was furious. Frustrated by his lack of practice that didn't come close to trumping his desire, his *need*, to feel Alexei in his mouth. In his throat.

Alexei's big hand stroked his cheek. "So eager. There's no rush."

Mike closed his eyes and nodded when Alexei's hand brushed his cheek again, soothed by his touch and the timbre of Alexei's deep voice. He forced himself to slow down, then tried again, worshipping Alexei's cock with his tongue. His lips. Figuring out what was manageable. Confirming what he loved about it—everything he'd thought he would, *and* the rude noises, the drool on his chin, the ache in his jaw—and set about discovering everything *Alexei* loved about it. The latter was trickier, but he thought he was learning to read the signs.

He wrapped a fist around Alexei's shaft and listened to him gulp air. He dug the tip of his tongue into the slit, and noted how Alexei shifted on his feet.

Throughout, a hand petted his hair. His cheek. Quiet murmurs of pleasure and encouragement flowed over him and he sped up, so the words came faster. Louder. Mike felt drunk with relief. With joy.

He was *finally* doing this.

"Take my clothes off."

Mike pulled off with a gasp and Alexei's strong hand at the back of his neck pressed his face to Alexei's belly. They both fought to catch their breath as Mike wrestled Alexei's jeans down his legs and licked any and every inch of skin he could reach.

Alexei toed off his shoes and kicked out of his pants, his shirt landing on top of the pile beside them. Mike wished he could have taken it off for him, but it was just as well Alexei had spared him having to stand up. Mike was pretty sure his legs wouldn't support him right now.

He stared at Alexei, naked, gorgeous, standing in front of him. Mike's hypersensitive fingertips skimmed over Alexei's long, strong legs, his thick thighs and perfectly round, rock-hard butt. Burying his face against the thatch of hair above Alexei's cock, his forehead pressed to the soft skin on his belly, Mike inhaled deeply.

Alexei groaned. "God, what you do to me."

The words were another caress. Another pleasure Mike stored away. Savored. He took Alexei's shaft in his mouth again, only this time, he kept a hand around the base as he worked up and down the length. He rubbed his tongue under the head, tickling the divot there, then plunged. Retreated. Soon Alexei had a fistful of his hair and was guiding his head. He didn't shove Mike down, though Mike sort of wished he would, gag reflex be damned, but he turned his head this way and that, sometimes smashing Mike's face to his belly to lick around the base of his shaft, other times holding Mike away so he could gently thrust just the head through Mike's lips.

"Jesus, Michael. So good."

Yes, it is. Mike's dick ached where it was bent in his pants, but he ignored it. He needed both hands on Alexei. Hell, he wished he had more than just the two. He had so many things he still wanted to try, to experience, he thought he might never get to them all in this lifetime, let alone today.

When the grip in his hair eased just a little, he pulled off Alexei's cock with a crude popping sound that made him smile. He lifted the shaft and eagerly licked his way down the underside but then paused and looked up at Alexei.

Alexei cocked one eyebrow, clearly understanding what Mike wanted. "Go ahead."

Mike opened his mouth wide against Alexei's firm sac and sucked the soft skin into his mouth. With a roll of his tongue, he eased one ball past his teeth and wrapped his lips around it.

Alexei hissed, "Holy shit," his voice a strangled mixture of laugh and groan. The hand in his hair curled into a tight fist again.

Mike hummed, intending only to indicate he'd heard.

Alexei shuddered under his hands. *"Fuck!"*

So Mike hummed again, leaning in when Alexei rose up onto the balls of his feet, his grip on Mike's hair eye-watering. He massaged Alexei's sac with his lips. His tongue. He'd seen this, read about it, but as with everything else he'd tried so far, the reality was so much fucking better. The salty taste, the even more intense musk, set his blood on fire. His poor cock, still trapped and at an ever-more unfortunate angle in his jeans, strained and ached.

He wrapped a hand around Alexei's big thigh and pushed it away. Up. Trying to lift it.

Alexei grunted above him. "What are you doing?"

"Please," Mike said, his voice muffled as he released Alexei's sac and nosed along the seam. He felt frantic. Pushed harder on Alexei's leg. It was awkward as hell, his neck straining, but Mike shoved his nose behind Alexei's balls and licked along his perineum.

Alexei froze, then Mike's head was yanked away by the fierce grip in his hair.

"If you're going to do it, let's do it right."

Mike's cheeks burned. "I don't know how," he admitted.

"Yes, you do. You were doing it better and with more enthusiasm than anyone else I've ever been with."

Mike felt his flush deepen at the compliment. Then he watched, wide-eyed, as Alexei turned, slid a knee onto the island counter, and spread himself open.

He'd seen Alexei go almost into a split in the goal, but this was just...*wow*.

Mike threw caution and every insecurity he had about his inexperience to the wind. If Alexei liked enthusiastic, he'd fucking get it. Mike buried his face against Alexei's ass, running his tongue the length of the crease and bumping over the knot of muscles before tickling the perineum again. He lavished his attention there, licking, sucking, biting as best he could, his hands clamped around the globes of Alexei's ass to spread him open and tilt him to Mike's mouth.

He had no idea what the hell he was doing, but Alexei clearly liked it. He shoved his ass into Mike's face, barking out orders that Mike gleefully followed.

At Alexei's command, Mike teased the tip of his tongue around the edges of Alexei's anus, soothing the muscles there. He'd done this with his fingers to himself countless times, but he was still amazed to feel Alexei's muscles easing. To hear Alexei shouting his approval.

He thrust a finger into his mouth, then pressed the tip right alongside his tongue.

"Put that finger in me, Michael. *Now.*"

Mike eased forward gently.

"Harder! Push it in!"

Mike shoved his finger deep into Alexei's ass and Alexei cried out something in Russian, his hips rocking. For one stunned moment, all Mike could do was stare at his finger plunging in and out of Alexei's ass.

He was perilously close to coming in his pants. "God, that's so hot," he breathed.

"Another."

"What?"

"Another finger, Michael. Now."

Mike did as he was told, his arm shaking, his head spinning. Alexei barked out orders, each one dragging Mike closer to the abyss. He thrust and scissored with his fingers, fucking Alexei exactly as he demanded.

Mike fucking *loved it.* Too much, it seemed. Without so much of a brush of a hand against his cock, he was losing it. "Shit, I'm going to come. I'm gonna—"

He gasped when Alexei grabbed his wrist and yanked his fingers out of Alexei's ass. Alexei grunted at their abrupt departure, then spun and took Mike's face in both his hands.

"You don't come until I tell you to. Understand?"

Mike nodded, his stomach knotted from the need that had been boiling there for what felt like hours. Being told he wasn't allowed to climax only brought him that much closer to the edge. Jesus, how did Alexei know how to push all his buttons?

"Yes," Mike said, his voice hoarse. "I understand."

Alexei held his upturned face and stared at him like he'd never seen him before.

"You really do want this," Alexei said, amazed.

"More than anything."

Chapter Eleven

Alexei was still having a hard time believing his eyes. What was right in front of him.

He knelt, his bare knees framing Mike's jean-covered legs. He couldn't seem to stop touching Mike's face. Kissing him gently. Licking into Mike's mouth before dancing their tongues from one mouth to another. Mike never tried to take control. He just...followed.

Which was all the more remarkable, and sweet, because Alexei knew he could stop and toss out any number of topics that got Mike's back up, and his friend would argue with him until he was blue in the face.

Alexei had the sinking suspicion that he was an idiot. He'd always been attracted to a particular kind of man. He admired strength and toughness, both physical and mental. Traits he found frequently among hockey players—often to his dismay. And from these men he'd sought out lovers who were not just submissive in the bedroom, but who'd been willing to carry that submission over to all other aspects of their relationship— until they couldn't do it anymore and left.

Now, looking down into Mike's flushed face, he felt incredibly stupid. Mike waited quietly for Alexei. No doubt eager to do whatever Alexei asked—just as Alexei had always wanted in a lover. And when they were done, they would argue about dinner. Or who should do the laundry. Or whether or not Alexei should have let that goal in the second period get past him.

And *that*, Alexei realized with a terrifying mixture of shock and excitement, was what he *really* wanted.

What, apparently, Mike wanted too. Alexei took in how Mike's hair stood on end from Alexei's fingers. His eyes bright with arousal. He'd never looked more handsome. Or so debauched. Alexei glanced down at the rigid line of Mike's erection straining against his jeans.

"Does that hurt?"

"Yes."

"Why didn't you adjust yourself?" Alexei wouldn't have been able to resist freeing his dick and probably jerking off by now, had the situation been reversed.

"You didn't tell me to." He said it like it was obvious, with just a hint of sass in his smirk.

Alexei smiled. Kissed him again. Longer and harder this time.

"Come to the bedroom," Alexei said, rising to his feet. He reached down to take Mike's hand and helped him to stand.

Alexei had only been on his knees for a few minutes and they ached. Mike didn't so much as wince.

Alexei's heart beat so hard, it felt like it was banging against his ribs. That was probably why he couldn't draw a deep breath when he looked at Mike. Why his chest ached.

He laced their fingers together, led Mike down the hall to his bedroom, and stopped just inside the door. He'd never brought another man here before. And he was glad.

"Take off your clothes," he said as he released Mike's hand and walked farther into the room.

He heard the sound of fabric rustling behind him and smiled.

"Go lie down on the bed."

Mike slid past him and was halfway onto the tall king mattress before Alexei recalled the other night and Mike's shameless presentation of his ass in the air. His cock twitched and his smile grew.

"On your back, Michael."

Mike paused in the process of planting his face against the mattress and flipped onto his back.

Alexei sat on the edge of the mattress. "We won't fuck tonight," he said, mindful of Mike's inexperience. If Alexei had known then what he knew now—

"We won't?" Rather than reassured, Mike appeared to be disappointed.

"You're probably sore."

Mike smiled. "I am. A little."

"Then we will find other entertainments," Alexei promised, his mind pretty much reeling through the possibilities like an X-rated slide show.

He was yanked back to reality when a hand landed on his arm. He blinked, then stared down at Mike, momentarily shocked again to see the gorgeous defenseman stretched out across his bed.

Mike said, "We can do whatever you want," but then he seemed to hesitate.

Alexei was instantly wary. "I like to be in charge, Mike, not an asshole. Tell me what's on your mind."

"I like being sore."

Some men hated it, but Alexei couldn't pretend to be anything but delighted that Mike wasn't one of them. His adults-only slide show was getting longer by the second.

Mike's eyebrows drew down, and his color edged toward pink. Embarrassed?

Alexei gripped his arm. "The truth, Michael."

"I like *fucking* when I'm sore."

Alexei battled a fresh surge of lust trying to cripple his higher brain function. "I don't understand. You said I was your first."

"You are."

"Then explain."

"When I would play, you know, by myself, I liked it when I was already sore." With every word Mike spoke, he turned a

112

shade pinker, but he didn't falter. "I'd think about you, and what it would be like to feel you like that, and I liked it better—"

Alexei pressed an unsteady finger to Mike's lips, silencing him. "Did you really think of me? When you fucked yourself?"

Mike didn't look away. "Yes."

"With that monster in your drawer?"

"Yes. Sometimes."

"I'm not that big, Michael."

Mike's cheeks glowed red. "No, but you're better."

"How?"

"Alive. Warm." His lips quirked. "You move of your own volition."

Alexei chuckled. "I see your point." He ran a hand down Mike's chest and tried not to laugh out right at how his knees bent and spread the closer Alexei's hand came to his cock. He gripped the hard shaft in his hand and Mike planted his feet wide on the bed. "This feel more warm and alive than your own hand?"

"No," Mike admitted with a quick inhale and a wobbly smile. "Just...*better.*"

Alexei stroked the smooth length once, then slid his hand between Mike's legs. His knees fell open onto the mattress.

So damn flexible.

Mike flinched when the pad of one finger stroked across the tender hole in question. Alexei forced himself not to think too long about how tight and hot it had been. Just because Mike said he liked it, didn't mean Alexei was going to leap on the damn man.

"Sore, huh?"

"Yes." A bead of pre-come dripped from the head of Mike's cock onto his stomach.

Jesus. Alexei pressed harder. Mike squirmed, his eyes wide and unfocused.

Alexei stilled. "Michael, if I do something you don't like, you have to tell me."

"Okay," Mike said in a hoarse voice, his ass twitching against Alexei's hand. "Do I need a special word or something?"

"No."

"No?"

"No. That's your special word. It's very simple with me. If you say no, I stop. If you say stop, I stop. If you have questions, ask them and we won't go on until they're answered."

Mike blinked, his vague gaze clearing. "I—Okay. That's good."

Alexei smiled, pleased and reassured that they both understood the ground rules. Then he looked down to where his fingers pressed against the still slightly red and swollen ring of Michael's anus. It wasn't too bad, but it also didn't look comfortable—and Mike clearly loved it that way.

Something snapped in Alexei. Some thin tether he'd still clutched, grounded in the disbelief that Michael could truly want what Alexei wanted and still be his stubborn, hard-headed best friend.

He dug the tips of his fingers against the hot flesh ringing Michael's entrance and smiled when his friend gasped and arched against the bed.

"Get on your knees."

Michael did it so fast that Alexei wasn't certain he hadn't levitated.

His eyes never left Michael's beautiful ass, tilted up to his view above the long stretch of Mike's back. Alexei reached for a condom and the lube from the bedside table. Mike shivered at the sound of the foil packet tearing. Whimpered when the bottle made a rude sound. Alexei thought someday he might torture Mike like this for a while, just with sounds and his shifting weight on the mattress.

Mike was so beautifully responsive. Completely without

guile. It was more than a little terrifying. And totally fucking hot.

"Grab the headboard."

Shoulders and neck muscles bulging, ribs expanding with every pant, Michael clamped onto the headboard, spread his knees, and held himself there.

Waiting for Alexei.

Alexei gave into his long-suppressed desire and planted his teeth against the soft curve of Michael's ass.

He bit his lover. Hard.

A grunt tore from Michael's throat, his body jerked, and one arm disappeared beneath his chest. Alexei pinched the perfect flesh between his teeth—an even sharper nip that elicited a loud yelp—then sat up.

He slid his hand between Michael's legs and over the fist clutching the base of Michael's shaft.

"You let go of the headboard."

"Sorry," Michael gasped. "Was going to come."

Alexei thought it was probably good that Michael couldn't see his grin. Or his hand swinging to connect with his ass, right over the blooming red bite mark.

Michael jerked, his knuckles going white.

Alexei would have spanked him again, but he was starting to fear Michael might rip his junk right off rather than betray Alexei's command.

Now Alexei had to grab *his* dick to wrestle his own orgasm back.

His hand came away covered in lube, and he drew it down the crease of Michael's ass. He didn't hesitate to thrust one finger past tender, red flesh and into Michael's body.

His lover shuddered. "God, Alexei. That feels so fucking good."

Mike thought he probably ought to be embarrassed at the way Alexei was making him carry on, but he couldn't stop. His aching muscles clung to the slow drag of Alexei's finger, unable to relax. His skin achingly sensitive to Alexei's every movement. Every touch.

Alexei slid a second finger in next to his first, this one loaded with lube. He pressed against stinging skin, eliciting an endless string of hisses and grunts. Mike's eyes swam with unshed tears. His hands trembled where they gripped the bed and his own dick.

It was so good. Way better than anything he'd ever been able to shove up his own ass.

Alexei's lips skimmed over the base of Mike's spine and he groaned, biting his lips to keep from blurting out what he was feeling. Not in his ass, which was fucking spectacular. But in his head. His heart.

Then Alexei's fingers were gone. Mike looked back, over his shoulder, and barely saved himself from an undignified face-plant by gripping the headboard with both hands again.

Alexei ran a hand up and down Mike's back, soothing him, until a palm dug into the stinging bite mark on his ass. A smile hovered on Alexei's lips as he reached for the lube. He didn't pause, or hesitate, or warn Mike in any way before spreading his ass open and pouring a ton of the stuff into him.

Mike gasped. "Now I know why you buy it by the gallon."

Alexei laughed. "That cheap shit is only for pranks. I would never risk your comfort with that, Michael."

God, he loved the sound of his name on Alexei's lips. How Alexei switched to calling him Michael only when they were like this.

Then Alexei was there, his cock pressing against the screaming muscles and fiery skin of Mike's ass, and he no longer could have told anyone his *own* name, let alone what anyone else called him. He gripped the headboard so hard his fingers ached, tilted his ass higher, and closed his eyes.

The burn. The stretch. It was magnificent. The moment of exquisite pain and pleasure when the wide head popped inside. The slick glide of thick shaft easing deeper and deeper into his body with each small thrust.

Mike was lost to the fire and ecstasy storming through him.

He moaned, acutely aware of the soft skin of Alexei's belly as it came to rest against his ass. He thought he could feel every tiny hair brush against the bite mark and where his ass still glowed from Alexei's spank.

He only wished Alexei had spanked him more. Harder. So he could feel *more.*

"You okay?" Alexei's voice was low and rough, his hands gentle as he rubbed Mike's spine.

"*Yes.*"

"You sure?" A finger traced the muscles stretched around Alexei's cock.

Mike shivered, clamping down around Alexei's shaft and making the burn a hundred times worse. And better.

"Yes. It feels good. *You* feel good. Now, please, please, *please* would you fuck me?"

Alexei's chuckle lulled him, then two strong fingers pinched the skin still throbbing from the bite.

Mike yelped and jerked back hard, shifting Alexei inside him. *Fuck.* He threw back his head and slammed his eyes shut, choking on his need to scream and beg for more.

Alexei wrapped his arms around Mike's chest, and Mike strained to hold both of their weight above the bed. Soft lips brushed his ear, but said nothing.

Alexei ground his cock into Mike's ass and slowly rolled his hips, jamming his rock-hard shaft against aching walls and burning muscles.

"How's that?"

"Good," Mike gasped, beyond the ability to string two words together.

Alexei ground harder. "And that?"

"Amazing."

"Not too much?"

"No." God, no. He wanted more. He wanted whatever the hell Alexei could dish out.

Which, it turned out, was a whole hell of a lot.

Alexei lifted off of Mike's back and wrapped his hands around Mike's waist. Mike held his breath and prayed to god that he would be able to hold out for more than three thrusts before breaking his promise to Alexei and blowing all over the sheets.

Alexei withdrew slowly, each excruciating inch singing along Mike's fluttering muscles, the lube easing the friction but not nearly enough to erase the sting. Thank god.

Then Alexei threw himself forward, penetrating Mike to the hilt, the thick base of his shaft stretching Mike wider. Better.

Mike howled his approval.

He clung to the headboard with all his might while Alexei fucked him hard and deep, relentlessly. His arms burned. Shook. He was making an absolute racket and he didn't give a shit. They had no neighbors and if Alexei was going to fuck him like this on a regular basis—*please god*—they probably should never get any.

Mike's throat burned but he couldn't stop shouting Alexei's name. And *good*. And *yes*. And *harder*. And *more*.

"More?" Alexei asked, breathless and fierce, not slowing his thrusts.

"Yes. God, fuck, yes."

Mike didn't know what the hell more could possibly be.

"*Fuuuck!*"

More was Alexei shoving a thick finger into Mike's ass alongside his cock.

Then a second finger.

And a third.

The searing stretch wrenched a constant bellow of joy from Mike. He felt raw. Open. Defenseless.

Happy.

Alexei twisted his hand and three soft finger pads strummed over Mike's sweet spot.

Mid-scream, Mike went dead silent, his mouth open in a silent roar, his eyes screwed shut, leaking tears.

"Come now, Michael."

Honest to god, Mike didn't just come. He came unglued.

Chapter Twelve

By the time of the Ice Cats reached the division finals two months later, there were very few places on Mike's body that weren't sore. Play-off hockey, at any level, was brutal, and there had been no exceptions this year. Mike had been slammed to the boards so many times, he felt like one big bruise.

And then there were the good hurts. The ones from Alexei.

He could feel two fresh bruises on his ass. Alexei hadn't been kidding. He couldn't stop biting him. There had been an awkward moment in the locker room after the first time, for which Mike was still getting a ton of shit from the guys. He'd since perfected the art of keeping his ass covered almost all the time, and Alexei had learned to tuck his nips lower, in the crease between his ass and thigh, or better yet, higher, in the tender flesh of his thigh just behind his balls.

Alexei had once suggested he stop leaving marks for the rest of the post-season, but Mike had successfully talked him out of it.

Thank god.

Mike shifted against his hard chair and used the unexpectedly fancy restaurant's linen napkin to mask the small, delighted twitch of his lips. He thought anyone in the room should be able to look at him and know. They would see the wince, the smile, the way he fidgeted on his seat, and recognize a well-fucked, happy man.

Except, of course, for his clueless parents sitting right across the table from him. Beside him, Jayne kept sending him questioning glances, but Mike was entirely confident his family would go on seeing only what they wanted to see. Believing only what they wanted to believe.

He didn't care so much. Not anymore. His life was in Moncton, and this visit was just a quick meal after their game that night. He was glad his family had come to watch them win, was happy to catch up about aunts and uncles and cousins and neighbors. And he would be perfectly content when, come morning, his parents got in their car and headed for home.

Jayne was staying a little longer, and Mike was thinking, just maybe, he could tell her about—

"Mike, did you hear? Kevin Miller is getting married this summer," his mother announced.

Jayne rolled her eyes and Mike fought the urge to join her. "Good for him."

"Beatrice—you remember his mother?—is *so* pleased. He found a lovely girl. They're already talking about having children."

Of course they are. He had to look away from Jayne's sympathetic look, leaving him with the choice of looking at his plate or his mother. His asparagus looked delicious. "That's great."

"And Cassidy, down the street? She just had her *third* child. Those kids are running their grandparents ragged," his mother said with blatant envy.

Mike smiled wanly and wondered how many times he was going to repeat the words, "That's great."

She continued on, completely oblivious, as usual, to her son's mood and the dozen more times he offered his stock, monotone answer. Babies. Weddings. His mother was *obsessed.* And about as subtle as a brick.

"...and that should be some wedding! Too bad we can't go, but of course, I already let your Aunt Mary know that we'd all be coming to Brian's wedding. And Erica's due in June, so I'm guessing there'll be a baptism sometime in July. Maybe August."

Mike couldn't take it anymore. The months stretched

ahead of him like the eight circle of hell. He blurted out, "I won't be home this summer," before he could think better of it. He and Alexei had been talking about it, but with the play-off travel schedule and general exhaustion, no decisions had been made. Now, he could see there had never really been a decision to make.

His mother's litany of domestic bliss finally came to a halt. "What? At all?"

"No. Sorry. I'm working. You know, for Alexei." Just saying his name should have made Mike feel better, but the lie made him feel vaguely ill. Alexei wasn't his boss. And Mike wouldn't allow Alexei to pay him any longer. He had no idea how the hell he was going to find money to send home this summer. "I'll see if I can make it to Brian's wedding," he added as a concession. It wasn't his cousin's fault he was straight and Mike's mother was fucking baby crazy.

"Don't be ridiculous, Mike. We can find you a job. And I have too much planned for you to flake out on us."

Mike willfully ignored the flaking out comment. "You do?"

"Yes. A few of my friends at church and I have been talking and they'd love to introduce you to their daughters. Oh, and one of them has a niece that we think would be just perfect for you. I was thinking you could—"

"No!" Mike said loudly, then took a deep breath and choked back the desire to continue shouting. "Mom, please, listen to me. I don't want you to fix me up with anyone. I don't want to get married, okay? Just *stop*."

His mother sucked in a breath like he'd punched her in the stomach. "What?"

His father chuckled. "Easy, Louise." He sent Mike a conspiratorial smile. "I'm sure at twenty two, Mike still has some wild oats to sow."

He sure as hell did, but that didn't make his father's comment any less creepy. Jesus. "Actually, I think you should count on the fact I'll never find a girl I want to marry."

And that was as close to the absolute truth as Mike had ever come.

His mother looked stricken. His father confused.

"Dad!" Jayne said, her voice sounding overloud in the stunned silence around the table. "Tell Mike about your new job. You were saying it's kind of fun?"

Mike's father visibly pulled himself together, even managing a weak smile. "Yeah. It's a good group of guys. They're all younger, of course. Lots of energy, but I try to keep up."

Mike winced. He appreciated Jayne's obvious attempt to change the subject, but she'd managed to land them on Mike's second least favorite topic—the lasting evidence of how launching Mike into hockey had decimated his father's career in the process.

"That's great, Dad," Mike said, trying to drum up genuine enthusiasm. "You working the day shift?"

His dad shrugged. "Nah. Just part time. Nights. But I'm hoping to get more hours, eventually. And it all helps."

Mike felt a familiar rush of frustration as he imagined how much of his pay would be going home for years to come. Predictably, it was followed by a tidal wave of guilt. This was his fault, even if he hadn't signed up for any of it.

"I'm sorry to hear that," he managed. "I'll see what I can do about sending more home, okay?"

"Thanks, son."

"No!"

Their parents both looked at his sister like she'd lost her mind. Mike guessed he was, too.

"I can take out loans," Jayne said firmly.

Mike frowned at his sister. "It's okay, I want to—"

"No." Jayne stared right at Mike. "I'm sorry I didn't figure it out sooner, that my tuition was a problem. They never told me."

"What your mother and I decide is necessary to keep this family afloat is none of your affair," their father said in his patented *shut up now or there'll be hell to pay* voice.

"I disagree, Dad," Jayne stated flatly.

Mike had to admire her guts, even as he wished she'd let it go. He wasn't going to let her take out loans any more than his parents were. He shook his head at her discreetly, begging her silently to drop it, but she ignored him.

"It's not fair to Mike. Lots of people get loans—"

"That's enough, Jayne," their dad barked, striking the table with his fist. "This family sacrificed to get Mike where he is, and now it's his turn. *He owes us.*"

And there it was.

Mike wasn't the least bit surprised, but still his meal curdled in his stomach as they all sat, silent, and absorbed what his father had finally admitted aloud. Mike owed them. Money. Babies. His willingness to slip into the life they'd carved out for him, without his input, regardless of whether or not he wanted anything to do with it.

Mike stood and carefully placed his napkin beside his plate.

He felt sorry for Jayne and the horrified realization written all over her face. Even felt sorry for the disgusted twist to his mother's mouth and her obvious distaste at having such matters discussed at the dinner table. In public, no less. He didn't bother to check what expression his father wore. Mike didn't want to hear whatever else he might like to add.

They'd all said enough for one night.

"Thank you for dinner. And for coming down to see the game," he said to the centerpiece, and then to Jayne.

Jayne started to stand, but he put a hand on her shoulder and squeezed. She looked furious, but he could tell it wasn't for him. He'd catch up with her later. Make it right between them.

But right now, he just needed to leave.

Without a backward glance, he left the restaurant and started walking toward the hotel.

Alexei sat on the edge of his hotel room bed for hours, twitching at every sound in the hallway, waiting for Mike to come back.

Alexei had been anxious about this visit, and Mike's meal out with his parents after the game, for the two weeks it had been in the works. Mike, though, had seemed okay with it. Tonight, he'd been just as Alexei had come to expect after they'd won a big game. Happy. Relaxed. His smile had only dimmed a little when he'd announced he had to head out to meet his parents.

It was such a radical departure from how Mike had been just five months ago at Christmastime, Alexei had let himself stop worrying for a while. Mike had changed. Become more confident. More settled with who he was, in so many ways. He'd certainly taken to debating things with Alexei with a new passion that Alexei adored, even if it made him a little crazy, too.

But now, sitting here waiting, Alexei couldn't shake the feeling that Mike seeing his parents would take all that away again.

Alexei wished he'd gotten his shit together sooner and told Mike his ideas for the summer. For the future. He realized, in hindsight, he'd been a coward. And because of that, he'd sent Mike off to the wolves without protection.

The sound of a key in the door brought him to his feet, his hand on the knob, pulling the door open, before Mike had a chance to enter the room.

All of Alexei's fears were realized, stamped on Mike's pale face. The light was gone from his eyes. The achingly vulnerable man Alexei had met on Mike's first day in Moncton—a man Alexei hadn't seen in months—had returned.

He towed Mike into the room, closing the door as he wrapped his arms around Mike as tightly as he dared this far into the play-offs.

"You're okay," Alexei said, his lips pressed to Mike's neck.

Mike clung to Alexei, his hands tight fists against Alexei's back, and shook his head.

Alexei ran a hand up and down Mike's back, trying to soothe him. It made no difference. He buried his nose in the soft skin behind Mike's ear, pressing his lips to the frantic pulse beneath. Ran his fingers through Mike's hair. Rubbed his neck. His back. Mike held on, painfully tight, but remained rigid. Unbending. Alexei's responsive lover was lost.

In desperation, Alexei glided a palm over Mike's ass, intimate knowledge and lots of practice allowing him to unerringly find the freshest bite mark. Testing, he pressed two fingers into Mike's flesh.

Mike shuddered, and melted against Alexei like his strings had been cut.

"What happened, Michael?" Alexei asked quietly, letting a hint of command thread through his voice. They didn't often take these roles outside of sex. Almost never, in fact. But Alexei would do whatever it took to make Mike whole again. To help him eject whatever poison was eating him up inside.

Mike's voice was muffled against Alexei's shoulder. "He said I owed them," he began, telling Alexei what had happened, about the wife and grandchildren and financial stability he was expected to provide.

Alexei's jaw hurt from clenching his teeth so hard, but he held on and listened helplessly while Mike poured out the entire story.

By the time Mike finished, he was breathing hard.

Alexei waited until Mike had settled a little before he

spoke. "What do *you* want?"

Mike lifted his head so that Alexei could finally see his face. His color had returned some, but mostly in the form of damp cheeks and red-rimmed eyes. "What?"

"Do you want to marry a woman? Have ten grandchildren for your mother to show off at church?"

Mike actually shuddered. The look of utter revulsion on his face would have been comical in other circumstances. "*No.*"

"So, what?"

Mike stared at the wall over Alexei's shoulder as he gave it serious thought. "I don't want to go home this summer," he began thoughtfully.

They'd both already known this. "And?"

"I don't want to send them so much."

"And?"

"I want to keep enough to start saving."

"Good idea."

"And to help Jayne get through school."

"Okay."

"But I want to do that directly. Not going through my parents."

Alexei nodded. Because it was a good idea, and because he could feel more tension ease from Mike each time he spoke. "And?"

"And..." Mike repeated, focusing on Alexei's face with the first hint of a smile. "You."

"What?"

"I want *you.*"

Alexei smiled, towing Mike closer, pressed against his chest once more. Most of what Mike wanted, needed, he'd have to get for himself. Alexei would support him however he could, but ultimately, it was up to Mike.

But his last request? That, Alexei would freely give.

Chapter Thirteen

Mike woke up the next morning and couldn't remember where he was. He pried open one eye to see unfamiliar shapes and shadows. Felt the coarse sheets under his cheek.

Then the arm around his waist tightened, warm lips and bristly play-off beard brushed the back of his neck, and half the weight of a professional hockey goalie smashed him into the mattress.

Mike slipped back into half-sleep.

Yesterday had been an emotional roller coaster, but none of that mattered as much as the next ten minutes, floating here with Alexei wrapped around him. They had some magazine interview thing they had to get to at some point. One he should care about at least a little, he thought with a smile. He spared the clock a glance and saw they still had hours.

Mike waited, vaguely recalling some of the best moments of the last two months. His growing erection dug into the mattress, but he didn't touch it, instead savoring the discomfort. Alexei sometimes made him wait ages, and god, it was so fucking worth it.

More blood surged south.

The hand on his belly slid down and gripped his hip.

"*Moi milyy.*"

Mike smiled into his pillow. Alexei didn't know it, but Mike knew what it meant now.

My sweet boy.

Mike wondered if the helpful Russian left winger from Charlottetown who'd translated it for him would catch on if Mike asked him how to say *my sexy, brilliant man* in return.

Probably.

"Good morning," he murmured.

The warm hand traveled from his hip over his ass. "Are you sore?"

Mike's smile grew. "Yes."

Alexei had fucked Mike hard last night, still only a foot inside the room, on the same spot Mike had told Alexei about his horrible family. He'd smashed Mike against the door and shoved two fingers up his already tender ass, thumping his prostate until he'd barely been able to contain his shouts of joy. Only their teammates' voices in the hallway, their presence in the rooms around them, had held him back.

It had been exactly what he'd needed.

Alexei prodded at the now aching ring of muscles with one finger and Mike gasped, writhing.

"Poor baby," Alexei crooned in his ear, his sympathy genuine, but Mike could hear the smile there, too. "I can feel how swollen you are."

His thick finger wiggled past Mike's muscles without any lube and Mike gurgled into the pillow.

Alexei knew, without a doubt, that he could have Mike again, right now. Hard and fast. Slow and gentle. It would hurt either way and Mike would not just allow it, he'd want it. Need it. *Love* it.

But Alexei had no desire to hurt Mike. Not really. He liked to leave his mark, of course, but he would never do anything that would truly injure his lover. And after last night, *and* the night before, it would be too much.

He sucked in a deep breath, his mouth still pressed to the back of Mike's neck, and let the heady and familiar scent fill his head. He'd become addicted to this. To Mike.

It still scared the shit out of him, but his fear was nothing in the face of what he truly wanted. For Mike, he would be brave.

He gently circled the inflamed skin with his finger, feeling Mike clench around him, knowing that each clench set off a zing.

Mike made the most amazing noises when he was aroused. When they were home, Alexei's ears often rang for hours after they'd made love. When they were on the road, forcing Mike to contain that noise had become a favorite form of entertainment for them both.

Michael shuddered, wordlessly begging for more, his pillow muffling whimpers and groans.

This morning Alexei wanted to do something different.

He pulled his finger free and rolled off Mike. "Get the lube and a condom."

Mike jumped to his knees and reached over the side of the bed, leaving Alexei a perfect view of the swollen, fire-red ring of Mike's anus. The hairs on Alexei's neck stood on end when he considered what his dry finger must have felt like. Then Mike turned, supplies in hand and his cock as hard as a pike.

Alexei smiled. "Put them on."

Mike reached for Alexei's erection.

Alexei stopped him with one hand. "Put them on *you*."

Mike's head snapped up. His mouth fell open.

Alexei burst into laughter.

"Were you kidding?" Mike asked with a frown.

Alexei's laughter died instantly. He rolled to his knees and took Mike's face between his palms, furious at himself for putting that look of uncertainty on Mike's face.

"No, Michael," he said softly, "I'm not kidding." He kissed his lover, long and deep, slowly rubbing the tension from his shoulders. "I'm sorry for laughing. You just looked so surprised. I wasn't making fun of you, only enjoying the moment."

"Are you sure?"

"About teasing you or about the sex?"

"The sex," he said in a hoarse voice.

"Yes. I'm very sure. Now, hurry up and get ready. We don't want to have to rush the rest of it."

Michael sat back on his heels and tore open the little foil packet. Shaking hands attempted to put the condom on three times before Alexei plucked it from his fingers.

"Let me."

"Yes, please," Mike agreed with a little laugh. "I don't know what's wrong with me. I never have a hard time getting one on you."

Alexei smiled, stoutly refusing to chuckle at Michael's wide eyes. He looked elated and terrified as he watched Alexei roll the condom down his rigid shaft, then drench his cock in lube. He didn't even flinch as the cool liquid ran down over his waxed-clean bare skin.

Perhaps Alexei should have given Michael more time to consider. "You don't have to do it."

"What?" Mike's head snapped up. "I want to."

"You sure?"

He attempted a smile, but it wobbled badly. "Very sure."

Alexei searched Mike's face, relieved to find the growing light of determination, even while looking forward to reminding his lover just who was in charge, even from the bottom.

He turned and dropped to his elbows on the bed. "Prepare me."

For the span of a few heartbeats, there was not a single movement from behind him, not even so much as the mattress shifting. Alexei wasn't entirely certain Michael was still breathing. Then long, warm thighs slid between his, spreading his knees wider, and a single finger traced down the ticklish crease of his ass.

He gripped the sheets in his hands, refusing to squirm, and resorted to what came naturally. Giving orders.

"Hurry!"

Lube poured over his hole, caught up on fingers and rubbed into his skin. He'd thought he would let Mike take his time. He changed his mind.

"Put a finger in me. Now."

The stretch was good. Michael's groan relaxed Alexei more than anything his clever fingers were doing.

"A second."

A fleeting moment of burn passed quickly and Alexei gripped the bedding tighter. His cock bounced against his belly with every thrust. He bit the sheet between his teeth when Mike's fingers spread, scissoring wide.

They had played like this. Many times. But rarely did it go much farther before Alexei was throwing Mike to the bed and returning the favor, tenfold.

"Another."

For the first time, Michael hesitated, only for a second, but Alexei appreciated it when the third finger slid in and the burn returned, more intense this time. Tension coiled in Alexei's belly as Michael slowly worked the tight muscles.

The moment they eased, Alexei demanded more. "Harder. *Faster!*"

Soon he could hear Michael panting behind him. Feel how he unraveled through his grip on Alexei's hip and his gasps of pleasure.

Goddamn, Alexei couldn't wait another minute. He needed this. The stretch. The touch. This man inside him.

"Now, Michael. Do it now."

Mike stared down at Alexei's beautiful, round butt, and thought his heart might explode right out of his chest. He had all the permission he would ever need or get.

But he didn't want to do it like this.

As a rule—a rule he thoroughly enjoyed and thanked god for every day—he didn't call the shots when it came to sex. He had no illusions that just because their positions were reversed physically, they were also changed in any way mentally or emotionally. Or he sure as hell hoped not.

But just this once, he would make a request.

Leaning in, he whispered into his demanding lover's ear. "Turn over?"

Alexei turned his head, their noses almost brushing, and studied his face. Saw god only knew what in his eyes. Then rolled onto his back.

Mike's fingers slipped free.

"Thank you," he said softly, staring down at Alexei spread out before him. He clenched his hands into fists, trying to steady them. It was useless. They still shook.

"Come here, Michael."

As always, the lilt of Alexei's accent threading through his name sent chills down Mike's back. And soothed him.

Mike crawled over Alexei, their chests brushing, and stared down at the most beautiful face he'd ever seen. Alexei kissed him, drawing out their pleasure, replacing Mike's nerves with, if not calm, then a steadiness only Alexei could give him.

Alexei's knees came up to hug his ribs. "Go ahead, Michael."

He pushed forward and met more resistance than he anticipated. Maybe he hadn't prepared Alexei enough?

Alexei traced his thumb over the bumps between Mike's eyebrows. "Relax. It's just been a long time."

Mike stared into Alexei's steady green gaze, and rocked his hips forward. The head of his cock squeezed past taut muscles before locking into unbelievable heat.

His mouth fell open, and for a long moment, all sound

strangled off in his throat.

"Holy shit. You're so hot. So *tight*," he gasped when he finally had the ability to speak.

Alexei laughed. "Maybe you're just big."

Then he kissed Mike again. Long and hard. His firm grip on Mike's hips dragged him forward, further into heaven. Mike's eyes nearly crossed at the exquisite heat clenching his cock.

Soon he was working his hips in gentle circles, going deeper each time, their kisses becoming frantic as he picked up speed. Alexei's hands guided him, told him when to move, when he needed to stop, what worked, how hard.

It left Mike with nothing to do but *feel*. The tight grip of Alexei's body. The mind-numbing friction. He shuddered each time he thrust harder. Farther. When he hit Alexei's sweet spot, strong arms clung to him, holding him close.

Their kisses were endless. Madness. Mike could barely breathe, his pants escaping from their lips as their tongues warred and his body buzzed with each new sensation.

He was making love to Alexei.

He tore his mouth away with a hoarse gasp. The flood of oxygen only made him dizzier, happier, and the truth spilled from him, falling from his lips in time to his increasingly powerful and frantic thrusts.

"I love you. God, I love you. So fucking much."

Alexei looked up at Michael, his words winding through Alexei's head and heart, and taking root. He felt the same. Had the words to give back, but didn't think his lover, his friend, could hear them now.

Mike trembled against Alexei, his face flushed, his eyes wide and glassy. He was lost. Beautiful. Barely holding on.

Alexei was no better. The pure happiness of Michael's words worked magic in his brain. The sizzle and shock of

Michael's long, thick cock thrusting into him, nailing his prostate time and again, its own joy. One Alexei had forgotten he could feel.

If they'd been at home, he might have been shouting as loud and long as Michael ever had. As it was, his throat burned with choked-off cries and declarations.

He framed Mike's face in his hands, caught his soft brown gaze, and set him free.

"Come now, Michael," he whispered in a hoarse voice, the words no more than passing his lips before his own climax roared up and out him, coating his and Michael's chests.

Sore, well-used muscles clamped down around Michael's shaft as he slammed home and sobbed against Alexei's neck. His hips jerked, his body quaking so hard that Alexei had to hold on tighter, wrapping his arms and legs around him as best he could.

Chapter Fourteen

Mike still lay sprawled across Alexei's chest an hour later, practically humming from the feel of Alexei's fingers running through the hair at the nape of his neck. Once again, they'd made a complete mess of their bed, but fortunately, somewhere in this hotel, there was a second room with Alexei's name on it. They hadn't slept apart since their first night together, but they hadn't exactly shared with management that they could save on lodging costs either.

A loud knock on the door jolted Mike out of his silent musings.

"Mike? Are you in there? We've been trying to call." His father's muffled voice carried through the door.

Mike could feel the blood draining from his face.

"Mike?" Alexei whispered as he sat up, forcing Mike to do the same.

Mike blinked and looked at him. Frozen in place.

Another series of knocks rattled the door.

Mike didn't know what to do.

"Come on," Alexei said quietly, towing Mike from the bed. "Get dressed."

Right. Dressed. He moved silently, yanking on whatever clothes Alexei threw at him. Alexei quickly did the same, then scooped the condom wrappers from the floor and tossed the covers up over the bed. He went to the windows, only to discover they were bolted shut.

Fuck.

Alexei stood looking uncertainly at him, waiting for Mike to decide what to do. Could they pretend they weren't here? Wait for his parents to go away?

He could feel the color return to his face, cheeks hot, when he pictured cowering here for who knew how long. Making Alexei cower with him.

Fuck that. He straightened his shoulders, and surveyed the room. Then Alexei. He even looked down at himself. If there was a way to make it all presentable—which seemed unlikely—there was no getting around the fact that they, and the room, reeked of sex.

Which, actually, was fine. This was his life. He didn't regret a single decision that had led him to this place. To Alexei. And for once in his fucking life, he was going to *own it.*

He went to the door, pausing with his hand on the knob. He looked back at Alexei. "You okay with this?"

Alexei studied his face for a moment, then nodded. "I'm okay."

Mike smiled grimly, then opened the door.

Expecting to see only his father, Mike couldn't decide if it was better or worse that his entire family stood in the hallway. Maybe it didn't matter either way.

"You better come in," Mike said calmly.

They filed into the room and hovered by the closet while Mike closed the door behind them. He slid past his family and went to stand beside Alexei.

Jayne looked confused to the length of time it took her to examine his face, his rumpled clothes and wild hair, and to give Alexei the same once over. Then a bright smile split her face and she went to Alexei's other side to face their parents—neither of whom seemed to know where to look.

Mike had thought about this moment a lot over the past few years, but now that it had arrived, he felt remarkably calm.

"Mom, Dad, this is Alexei," Mike said.

His father finally looked at him. "Your boss?" he asked hopefully, no doubt grasping for an explanation for why Alexei was here.

"He was," Mike replied easily. "Now he's my boyfriend."

For a long time, no one said anything. Mike was actually pretty okay with that. He was enjoying a quiet moment of absolute fucking relief.

I did it. He'd come out to his parents, and while he suspected he'd once again botched it pretty badly, what with the trashed bed and the faint smell of latex and lube still in the air, he'd *done* it.

"I don't understand," his mother said at last.

Jayne huffed with obvious exasperation, but something about their mother's expression, the way her eyes darted around the room, held his attention.

"Yes, you do. You understand perfectly," he said with growing horror.

Mike studied his parent's faces, their reactions, and the lingering dread in his gut burned away, replaced by a hot rush of anger. His parents were nervous. Dismayed. But neither looked even a little bit surprised.

"Oh my god," Mike said softly, *"you knew."*

His father opened his mouth, probably to deny it, but Mike threw up a hand and shook his head. As if he could somehow ward off his parents' betrayal. All those women they'd thrown at him. The endless talk about marriages and babies. And they'd known.

How could any parents do that to their child? How could *his* parents do that to *him*?

Alexei pressed a hand to his back and Mike leaned against it. Taking the comfort and warmth it offered while Jayne stared at their parents, speechless. Alexei just looked up at Mike helplessly.

He turned back to his mother. "You made me fucking miserable. Do you realize that? Is that what you wanted?"

"No! Of course not. We didn't *know* anything," his mother said, but when Mike just stared at her, she looked away.

Mike's father sighed. "We thought you'd get over it."

"You thought I'd *get over it?*" Mike asked incredulously, trying to figure out where his parents had spent the last decade.

Alexei curled his hand in the back of Mike's shirt. Maybe he was as pissed off as Mike. Or maybe he was afraid Mike would bodily eject his parents from the hotel room. It *was* a really tempting thought.

"We thought that if we didn't encourage you, you'd let it go," Mike's father continued, apparently unaware he was a fucking idiot. "That you could change."

"I don't want to change!" Mike shouted, not even caring if the guys in the rooms around him heard. "I'm gay! I've always been gay. And what's more, I wouldn't change a goddamn thing if I could."

"Don't say that, Michael," his mother cried. "It's not—"

"It is! I seriously don't even want to know what you were about to say. This. *Is.* It's real and permanent and actually"—he put his hand out and Alexei immediately grasped it—"it's kind of great. Really great. You should be happy for me, Mom, because I'm happy. This is what I want. And that's all you should want for me."

They clearly didn't understand. Mike almost pitied them, but couldn't in light of what he'd learned.

He didn't owe them anything anymore.

"You know what? I think you should go."

"Go where?" his mother asked, and she seemed genuinely lost. His father looked equal parts confused and furious.

"Go home, Mom. Both of you. Think about it for a while, I guess. Figure out what you really believe. Whether you want to have me in your lives, exactly as I am. You know where to reach me if you do."

His mother blinked, her hand curled around the cross around her neck as she looked up at him. "But who will take care of you?"

"I can take care of myself," Mike said. It felt good knowing it was true.

"But Mike, everyone needs someone else to care about them. That's all we ever wanted for you. For you to have someone to love and who loves you."

"He has that already," Alexei said.

The pride and affection on Alexei's face took Mike's breath away. His heart galloped in his chest. "Really?"

Alexei smiled. "Yes, Michael. Of course, I love you."

Mike grinned. "Good. Because I love you, too."

"Okay, folks, I think that's our cue to leave," Jayne announced, skirting where Mike and Alexei still stood beaming at each other stupidly and herding their parents out the door. When their father opened his mouth to say something, Jayne cut him off. "You had your chance, Dad, and you blew it. Now you have to go home and think about your sad choices. Seriously. You know where to find Mike, but he asked you to leave, and frankly, I'm not going to let you do anything but respect that."

Their mother tried to admonish Jayne but her voice was cut off when Jayne closed the door in her face. Jayne turned back to Mike and Alexei.

"We're going out to dinner later," she announced.

"Okay. Meet in the lobby at six?" Alexei agreed before Mike could even open his mouth.

His sister crossed the room and pulled Alexei down until she could kiss his cheek. "Thank you."

Mike was delighted to watch the blush spread across Alexei's cheeks.

"For dinner?" Alexei asked.

"For everything," she answered. Then she kissed Mike's cheek too. "I'm happy for you, Mike."

141

"Thanks. Come visit, okay? In Moncton, I mean. Not here. In the hotel today. Because, umm...."

"Oh my god, Mike, stop talking," she begged.

Mike looked at Alexei helplessly, his face heating. Alexei just laughed at him.

"*Anyway*," Jayne continued, pulling out her phone. "I would love to come visit. Give me your new address."

Mike prattled off the street and number, finishing with, "Apartment 4B."

"4A," Alexei corrected.

Mike looked up at Alexei, a smile hovering on his lips. "Right," Mike said with a laugh, already trying to figure out how soon he could move. "I'll be in 4A."

Alexei smiled. "Right where you belong."

About the Author

Samantha Wayland has always dreamed of being a novelist. She wrote her first book as an escape from the pressures of her day job. That fascinating piece of contemporary erotic mystery/suspense with elements of paranormal, international intrigue, and god only knows what else, is safely tucked under her bed, where it will remain until hell freezes over. Since then, she's learned a lot about the craft and turned her attention to writing contemporary MM and MMF ménage erotic romance.

Sam lives with her family—of both the two and four-legged variety—outside of Boston. She used to spend her days toiling away in corporate nerdville but was recently sprung from that hell. Now when she's not locked away in her home office, she can generally be found tucked in the corner of the local Thai place with a few beloved friends (and fellow authors).

Her favorite things include mango martinis, tiny Chihuahuas with big attitude problems, and the Oxford comma.

Sam loves to hear from readers.

Email her at samantha@samanthawayland.com, or find her on Facebook as Samantha Wayland and on Twitter as @SamWayland.

Also by Samantha Wayland

With Grace

A man yearning to explore his sexual tastes but afraid to turn up the heat, the woman who loves him but is hungry for more spice...and the chef who craves them both.

When Grace, Philip and Mark find a mobster's flash drive full of incriminating information, they are quickly embroiled in a dangerous situation. They stay together for safety, but proximity ignites the sparks they've long been fighting to ignore.

When three friends dare to succumb to their appetites, they find the perfect recipe for love.

Destiny Calls

Patrick didn't think it would be a big deal to kiss Brandon, his best friend and fellow police officer. Hell, they'd done crazier things to escape a bar fight. But then he had no way of knowing just how hot it would be.

Destiny Matthews is not a woman who is afraid to ask for what she wants, and when she sees her two best friends kissing, she knows just what she's going to ask for. Before she can convince Patrick that he's not as straight as he likes to protest, Brandon is attacked by an unknown enemy.

While they fight to protect each other's lives, they prove time and again that they're even better at protecting their own hearts.

Fair Play

Hat Trick Book One

Savannah Morrison is the new athletic trainer for the Moncton Ice Cats, a professional hockey team in the wilds of New Brunswick. It's a good thing she's got plenty of knowledge and grit, because as the only woman trainer in the league, she has to work twice as hard to win the players' respect. The last thing on earth she would do is date one of them.

Twelve year hockey veteran Garrick LeBlanc isn't ready to hang up his skates, particularly since he hasn't figured out what the hell he's planning to do next. He needs the new trainer to keep him fit to play, and she's got the skills to do it. Too bad he lost his mind and hit on her the day they met. Now she hates his guts and he's made an art of ignoring her.

When the team is put up for sale, Garrick and Savannah have to work together to save their jobs and their team. Somewhere along the way, they discover Garrick isn't just a hockey player, Savannah isn't only passionate about her work, and just maybe they've got more in common than they thought.

Two Man Advantage

Hat Trick Book Two

Rhian is working his way up the ranks of professional hockey, with the dream of making it to the NHL getting closer every day. He's doing it alone—no family, no friends—and that's the way he likes it. Then he arrives in New Brunswick, and meets the Moncton Ice Cats. Suddenly, he's got friends—and even something that might be an honest-to-god crush.

Garrick is lonely and counting the days until his last season with the Ice Cats is over and he can move to Boston. When his girlfriend suggests he take a lover—as long that lover is a man and Garrick tells her all about it—he laughs it off. But damned if his buddy Rhian doesn't take on the starring role in his fantasies. Good thing Rhian is way too young—and straight—for what Garrick has in mind.

Rhian takes a chance when Garrick's increasingly confusing signals start making sense, and soon discovers he's bitten off more than he can chew. Sex with strangers is simple. Sex with his best friend? Complicated.

End Game

Hat Trick Book Three

Garrick LeBlanc never intended to fall in love with two people, but he has, and now he has to figure out what to do about it. He wants to make them happy, but is afraid he's doing just the opposite. To make matters worse, he's trapped in New Brunswick until the end of the hockey season, while his lovers are both in Boston.

Savannah Morrison has no one but herself to blame for practically shoving her lover into the arms of another man. After all, it was her idea that Garrick take a lover while they are separated for the season. She loves Garrick with all her heart, but how the hell is she going to share him with Rhian?

Rhian Savage used to have such a simple life. Now he's in love, his dreams of skating on an NHL team are coming true, and he keeps spotting a strangely familiar face in the crowds. To top it all off, he has to see Savannah every day. He knows she's Garrick's real future, but he doesn't have the balls to do the right thing for all of them and end it—until his life goes sideways. As usual.

Now Rhian is alone, Garrick is heartbroken, and Savannah—the one person Rhian figured would celebrate his departure—is beating down his door. What the hell is up with that?

CPSIA information can be obtained at www.ICGtesting.com
Printed in the USA
LVOW08s1015290316

481236LV00001B/31/P